DEATH-MADNESS

They had been in the air for forty-five minutes when the engines surged, palsied, then toned down. Sutton's stomach filled with that horrible sinking sensation, and he looked over at Zhuk. He would read Zhuk's face, not the instruments, because they were in undecipherable Russian. So it was Zhuk's face that took their place, and now it seemed calm, the bear's eyes reflecting no sense of emergency. Zhuk pointed down to an area ahead, perhaps fifty miles south in line with their heading. He had nosed the ship over and now they were losing altitude, the altimeter needle spinning backward quickly, Zhuk's big gloved hands holding the control wheel forward in his lap.

"Waffen-SS," Zhuk said, pointing again. "German troops. We bomb . . . strafe like this—" His left hand was palms up, indicating the ground, and the right was the Tu-2 coming along the palm at what seemed to be fifty feet off the ground. "Have you ever strafed troops?" Zhuk asked.

Sutton shook his head.

Zhuk unsnapped his oxygen mask and revealed a big smile. "Fun," he said.

IN SEARCH OF EAGLES
THE WINGS OF DEATH
#2

BY CHRISTOPHER SLOAN

ZEBRA BOOKS
KENSINGTON PUBLISHING CORP.

ZEBRA BOOKS

are published by

KENSINGTON PUBLISHING CORP.
475 Park Avenue South
New York, N.Y. 10016

Printed in the United States of America

In memory of my father, the Honorable Vincent A. Lupiano, for all our love left unsaid.

IN SEARCH OF EAGLES
THE WINGS OF DEATH
#2

You love a lot of things if you live around them. But there isn't any woman and there isn't any horse, not any before or after, that is as lovely as a great airplane. And men who love them are faithful to them even though they leave them for others. Man has one virginity to lose in fighters, and if it is a lovely airplane he loses it to, there is where his heart will forever be.

—Ernest Hemingway

Today I felt pass over me
A breath of wind on the wings of madness
—Charles Baudelaire

45th Bombardment Group (H)

Assigned Eighth Air Force: September 1942

Component Squadrons: 367th, 368th, and 444th
Bombardment Squadrons
(H)

Station: Bassingbourn, England, 7 December 1942 to
15 December 1945 (Air echelon arrived 8
through 14 September 1942

First Mission: 9 October 1942

Last Mission: 19 April 1945

Total Missions: 342

Total Credit Sorties: 9,614

Total Bomb Tonnage: 22,575 (248 tons of leaflets)

Aircraft Missing in Action: 171

Enemy Aircraft Claims: 332

Major Awards: One Medal of Honor (SSgt Richard
Jones—1 May 1945)

Two Distinguished Unit Citations

Five Legion of Merits

Twenty-two Silver Stars

Eight Hundred Distinguished Flying
Crosses

Sixty-five Bronze Stars

Five Soldier's Medals

Four Hundred and One Purple Hearts

Personnel Casualties: Killed in Action: 483

Missing in Action: 305

Wounded in Action: 145

Prisoners of War: 884

ONE

"We're over Paris," Gibson the navigator announced.

"Really?" Kid Kiley the rear gunner said, sounding genuinely surprised. "It looks like Washington, D.C."

"Maybe it is," replied Gibson. "Maybe this is all a bad dream."

On May 20th, a fine spring day, Captain James L. Sutton's B-17 Squadron had a raid on Orly Airfield in France. They would gather themselves up after a sad start and fight on to the other side of Paris, that beautiful city of lights that most of the American boys flying that day had never before seen.

Over Paris, rich in culture and history, bastion of fine food and wine, the citadel of stylish taste and handsome women, Sutton's crew would view the area like somber-faced tourists in a *Flying Fortress* they had reluctantly christened *The Beast;* and then, just a little further, where their ship would salvo a few tons of Yankee-brewed high explosives, negating for a moment everything wonderful and precious down there on this the finest day of spring in the year 1944. Of course going in and coming off the target there were fighter attacks and flak—"Just two minor hurdles," Corporal Bo Baker, the 24-year-old radio operator from Rhode Island said to Benny Tutone, the turret gunner from Brooklyn, before they climbed into *The Beast* on that fog-shrouded morning.

Orly, part of the Luftwaffe's Air Fleet 3, was commanded by the heavily jowled and flamboyant *Generalfeldmarshal* Hugo Sperrle, who had taken as his Paris headquarters the fabulous Palais du Luxembourg, one-time palace of Marie de Medici. Only a couple of weeks ago, on the 7th of May, *The Beast*'s crew barely missed killing Sperrle as he flew over France from a Knight's Cross ceremony in Berlin. Flying a top secret low-level mission, *The Beast* had set out to bring down Sperrle in his Junkers Ju52. Instead, they brought down three German aces flying guard for Sperrle—the aristocratic *Hauptman* Prince Ritter von Woll, who bailed out of his flaming FW-190; *Major* Hellmuth Hund, killed in the air by machine gun fire from Tutone's .50-caliber guns; and *Major* August Baerenfaenger, who crash-landed his badly damaged Focke-Wulf on a French road.

If today's mission to Orly was less spectacular than other raids Sutton's careworn crew had flown, the takeoff of thirty-six B-17s from their English airbase this morning was indeed terrible and extraordinary—a product of sun, vapor, and very bad luck.

The Orly raid did not begin over France. The run over the target was born hours before at 0400 at Bassingbourn, England, when the steely voiced Sergeant Litton came through Sutton's barracks banging his big flashlight with a drummer's precision. Litton, the human alarm clock: "Rise and shine, breakfast in half an hour, briefing at 0515." The act itself was innocent, but for many Litton would be the shadow of death summoning them toward fate. For those that lived through the 20th of May, the word *Orly* would have the same sharp sting as a sad song: in the future, memories would sparkle to life, a tiny time capsule that for many would come back to haunt them at the oddest times: driving a car, making love, gazing through the rainy window of a bus on a lonely road. *Orly:* A very sad memory on a fog-draped spring morning.

At 0550 Sergeant Benny Tutone and *The Beast*'s crew jumped from a truck and walked the short distance to their warmed bomber. Of the ten-man crew none was more eager to fly than Tutone. "Hey, boss," he said to Sutton, dropping his gear on the damp tarmac, "we gonna get us some Germans today?"

"Benny," Sutton said, cleaning his gold-rimmed sunglasses with a freshly pressed handkerchief, "you are definitely a hot case for a psychiatrist. You ask me the same damned question everytime we go off on a raid, and I always give you the same damned answer—we're going to end the war before dinner."

"All right, so I like to dream," Tutone said, reaching into his duffle bag.

"Tutone," said Roger Griffin, the world renowned blond-haired blue-eyed boy wonder copilot, "if this war ended you'd have nothing to live for."

"Yes, I would, Lieutenant." Tutone had his Kodak in hand and was motioning to the crew, positioning them for a picture under *The Beast*'s nose section.

13

"And what would that be?" Griffin said, his perfect smile primed for the shutter's click.

"Another war." He snapped the picture and the crew applauded, a nervous release, the nine of them caught smiling alongside *The Beast*'s olive drab snoot—the Bendix chin turret caught forever near the left frame of the photograph, the .50-calibers pointing skyward as if eager to get airborne. Above the crew's heads, the words *The Beast* had been drawn in bright yellow bubble-style letters outlined in bright red. Below, a green aardvark-like creature with a small set of stubby white wings had bullets spewing from machine gun-shaped nostrils.

An hour later, at 0655, serenity ended. The first of thirty-six 45th Bombardment Group *Fortresses* bound for sleepy Orly would come roaring down Bassingbourn's main runway. Each *Fort* had been armed with one-thousand M44 GP bombs loaded with 538 pounds of highly explosive Amatol, which, of course, knows no friendship. Once the tail and nose fuses on an M44 are set for detonation they know no distinction between friend and foe, error or purpose.

The Beast was the nineteenth bomber in line and Sutton, usually anxious during takeoffs, took three seconds to push the ganged throttles forward for full power. The four Wright R-1820-97 air-cooled engines throbbed; the ship sped true down the runway; the tail wheel rose; and a couple of seconds later the main gear came away and the bomber was airborne, cutting through the damp foggy air toward Orly. As they lifted, Roger Griffin noted the fog—the condition would hamper landings, but now the 45th was leaving England and by the time they returned the fog would be burned off by the sun's warm rays.

My Gosh! the twentieth aircraft in line for takeoff, failed to get airborne: a fuel pump problem in the number two engine. The pilot, Major Bob Fargo, stopped the aircraft halfway down the runway and turned back. Some of the crew were disappointed because this would mean one less mission to their credit; a few others were relieved, knowing they would not have to face flak and fighters today.

In *The Beast,* Kid Kiley glanced down from his gunner's tail position. "Hey," he announced excitedly on the interphone, "Fargo's taxiing back." Several seconds later *My Gosh!* was a faint outline below the fog's shroud.

The *Miami Momma* was the twenty-first in line that day. The pilot, Captain John Fuller, either did not have his radio tuned or had not seen the warning flares—he shoved the throttles wide open. His back pressed against the seat. The engines made their distinctive roar, a sound that cut through the hazy ground fog far beyond Bassingbourn's perimeters.

The air controller in the tower jumped from his seat.

"Jesus Christ!" he yelled, staring hard through a pair of binoculars. He barely saw the *Miami Momma* zooming down the runway but instinct told him what would happen; he dropped the glasses and screamed another futile warning into his microphone.

"What the hell's that?" the copilot of *My Gosh!* wondered aloud, referring to the sound of *Miami Momma*'s engines thundering directly toward him. Fargo peered through the windscreen.

In the next instant both pilots saw the unmistakable shapes of each other's aircraft.

15

Kid Kiley shook his head. "They're going to hit!"

"Oh God please," Fuller implored into his throat microphone, knowing there was no other source he could seek for help. His ship, still good and sound after thirty-three grueling missions, had not reached sufficient speed to bear him away from this looming insanity. The air passing over his ship's 103-foot wingspan did not provide the lift required to fly over the taxiing ship. The rules of physics and mass, of speed and distance and time, could not be disregarded—not even for this one special moment.

Fuller gave it his best shot, despite the horror that filled his young pilot's body. He acted through training, instinct, and in less than one second tried to save himself. His first action was to pull back hard on the control column, a totally insignificant effort. The *Miami Momma*'s big Goodyear tires remained spinning on the runway. Then Fuller acted through panic and fear because there were no alternatives—he brought his right forearm up over his eyes attempting to hide from the inevitable disaster. It was the last living thing he did.

Miami Momma slammed head-on into *My Gosh!* The result was a gruesome, cacophonous of sound. The explosive force of metal smacking metal shattered the still air with a fierce thunder that rolled across the meadows and fields like a horrible audible death. Front wing spars bent and twisted like strands of warmed plastic. The sky crowded with a confusion of airplane and human parts. Fuel transfer pumps, pieces of bulkhead, door motor and actuating mechanisms, chunks of instrument panels, thermos bottles, crew members' seats, machine guns and flailing prop blades splintered the air. A camera door flew wildly into the sky. Oxygen bottles and control cables mixed with bomb hoist brackets and showered the cement runway. A prop anti-icer tank went bouncing across the grassy infield like a steel medicine ball, spewing alcohol and glycerin in its path. Pieces of bodies were indistinguishable from pieces of airplane.

After impact the bomb bay hoist bracket in *My Gosh!* buckled and a one thousand-pound M44 shot forward like an unguided rocket. Zooming ahead, it severed the fuel transfer lines running horizontally across the Number 4 bulkhead that separated the cockpit from the bomb bay. The unforgiving M44's arming vane snapped loose and the nose fuse smashed into the armor plate and did what it was designed to do. The explosion kicked in, announced the end of the world. Over 500 pounds of Amatol triggered each of the one thousand-pounders in both aircraft. The force sent a shock wave with the temperament of a blowtorch rippling along the grass. Less than a mile away the air controller, stunned by the awesome sight and sound, was showered with snowed glass from the control tower's windows. The next *Fort* in line had a prop blade sheared by a piece of flying bomb rail.

Kid Kiley pressed his mike button. "They're gone." He watched the two bombers disappear in a ball of fire and smoke. A second later the shock wave fluttered out like a big smoke ring and *The Beast* quivered, struck by the ghost of death. "They're all gone."

Sutton and Griffin tried to glance back but it was difficult to see the runway; they listened to Kiley describe in droll tones what was happening.

Ahead, to the east, the sun shone, a golden cymbal

17

burning off the fog. Sutton thought of his friend, Dick Page, blown apart with his crew weeks ago when the *Mairzy Doats*' engines quit on takeoff five hundred feet above the runway. He stopped trying to look down and concentrated on flying. Twenty minutes later over France, Bo Baker received a radio report from Bassingbourn: twenty-one crewmen killed; half the bodies had vanished. One, Harley Everett, a freelance writer-photographer was up on his first B-17 flight. Age 27, a wife, one child. End of career.

No one in *The Beast* said anything for the next thirty minutes. They were pensive. Bo Baker tried to focus on a novel resting on his little table in the radio room; between the lines he thought about friends he had on the *Miami Momma*. Gibson checked the grease stains on his charts and picked his teeth with the cover of a book of matches. John "Chief" Whitefeather, one of the waist gunners, was pissed. Half of him felt glad to be alive, while the other half was angered over the stupidity of what he called *the fog deaths*. The Chief always gave objects and events mystical names, reading things into them that no one dared imagine. Amatol, the Chief thought, is supposed to be a friend—it is the stuff of war, sure, but it is on our side and shouldn't've blown like that. Most of the crew would have lived if the Amatol didn't blow. If . . . if they heard the warning on the radio . . . if they saw the flares . . . if the fog wasn't there . . . if the damned war never began in the first place. To the Chief the world seemed blurry—a lot of questions and very few answers. Maybe it was the altitude. Suddenly he felt lethargic, wanted to sleep forever. Anger does senseless things. He closed his eyes.

                    *   *   *

At 0845 that morning a German legend took off.

He was known as "the giant killer," and RAF and USAAF pilots did not know his name but they had his number—they knew him only as "Lucky Number 13."

His name was Georg-Peter Eder, a *major* in the Luftwaffe. His speciality was attacking American bombers head-on, a method considered suicidal by fellow pilots and American fliers as well. Preferring the head-on attack because the rapid closure rate gave American gunners minimum firing time with a maximum chance of missing him, Eder was one of the bravest fighter pilots ever to strap an airplane on his back. Wounded fourteen times, between 1940 and 1945, Eder shot down 78 Allied aircraft and was awarded the Oak Leaves to his Knight's Cross.

In March, 1942, Eder took command of Number 12 Squadron in *II Jagdgescwader 2,* flying with Richthofen Wing aces like Josef "Sepp" Wurmheller, Kurt Buehligen and Hans "Assi" Hahn. In February, 1944, Eder gained renown as the head-on *experten,* the airman that could successfully attack American heavies from the front. Flying with *Oberstleutnant* Egon Mayer, the *Kommodore* of JG-2, Eder perfected his head-on technique—thus taking on the aura of a living legend.

Initially, Tutone and the Chief both said that Number 13 was a Kraut trick, a psychological tool, that the Germans were sending up different pilots in different aircraft with the infamous Number 13 painted on the fuselage sides to confuse and frustrate Yankee gunners. The choice of the number itself was deliberate, the

Germans knowing it to be regarded as bad luck by all Americans.

"He's been shot at, shot down, and killed more than half a dozen times," Tutone snorted over a beer one night in London. The Chief nodded approval—but as time passed they agreed: only one man would either be brave enough or nuts enough to execute the treacherous head-on attack. Whoever he was, they held silent admiration for him. A few weeks later, the Group's intelligence officer, the humorous Richard Marks, briefed the assembled crews and gave them hard proof that demonstrated Georg-Peter Eder's existence. Suddenly the legend was alive.

This morning waiting ground crews had helped Eder and the other pilots into their cockpits, fastened the harness straps, started the engines, and removed the chocks so the FW-190s could sweep across the grassy airstrips and stab into the spring sky, tucking in their wheels the instant they came off the ground—a favorite conceit of all fighter pilots.

Brave and bold, frightened and reluctant—various emotions went with them as they climbed, listening to the vectors cracking in their headsets, making course corrections toward the 45th Bombardment Group, sweeping low across French farmlands in a *Schwarm*— a "finger four" formation. Eder glanced over at his wingman and gave a hand signal that said *nothing yet*.

Breaking radio silence, the wingman replied, "I'm in no hurry."

Over Pontoise the Chief tapped out the beat to *American Patrol* on the barrel of his .50-caliber machine gun, nestling it with his big arms, scanning the crisp spring sky, anxious to reach Orly and then wheel around for home. He had an odd feeling. The day had started badly, the sky was too calm—something awful would happen. The Chief was seldom wrong.

Tutone, as always, was thrilled to be up here today. The war gave him something to live for, something he never had on the streets of Brooklyn.

The bombardier, Rowe, the oldest crewman at thirty-three, was a career officer who'd been in the Air Force thirteen years and had been busted four times. Despite his dauntless veneer, Rowe's greatest fear was flying combat missions, something he never told anyone. A ladies' man, Rowe flew with four flak jackets tucked neatly around his groin. "A guy's gotta guard his weapon," he told Sutton, who angrily pointed to the .50-caliber guns on the Bendix chin turret Rowe was responsible for firing: *"That,* Lieutenant, is your weapon!"

If *The Beast* was anything she was her crew: her youth was represented by the smooth-skinned Kid Kiley, 18, fresh and eager and naive. Her mystery was Whitefeather, the Chief, and the answers only he could provide when nothing logical would suffice, when the crew yearned for answers only superstition could furnish. Her fear and panic, which they were entitled to, was Rowe and all the ineffable horror and paranoia he had wrapped in his skull and soul. Her naivete was embodied in Bush and Skolinsky, too virginal to have the others' fears. Her intellect was Baker, bookish, always questioning, distant. Gibson was their anguish, their doubt, a prayer for their success. Tutone was the guts and joy of the ship, the consummate hipster, overwhelmingly enthusiastic. Griffin, from a wealthy family, was their pride gone awry, their egotistical balloon on the verge of bursting at any moment. And their leadership was, rightfully, Sutton—levelheaded, clear-thinking.

The Beast was America—all the things America was and more; more than steel and wire, oil and gas, bullets and instruments. Socially, morally and intellectually, the crew was what America was: hope, fear, ambition, promise, pride. Most of all promise and hope. So if anything rode with them this fine spring day it was the doubt that the promise and hope of a whole nation might not live to see the sun rise the next day, that the crew would not live beyond today's mission. Each of them knew this and they kept it hidden like a child using a blanket to hide from the fear of a very dark night.

Rowe's terrible scream woke them and persisted until he was sure each of them shared his horror.

"Flak!" he kept yelling, until Sutton ordered him to shut up.

Now they were relieved because the expectation for battle was gone—it was here and they had to contend with it. Concentration filled each of them and brushed aside—at least for the moment—the fear of dying. They only had time now to think about living, and soon the fighters would be on them trying to burn them from the clear sky.

The Group was somewhere between Pontoise and Paris. Sutton looked down through air as clean as washed glass and saw the capital of France in the distance. A wispy smoke screen lay over the city, rippling on a gentle southwest breeze that moved almost imperceptibly.

At their altitude, 18,000 feet, the wind was west-by-southwest, 180°, almost a tailwind at 45 miles an hour.

The Chief spotted a formation of fighters sweeping up from below and behind.

"Hold your fire," Sutton ordered. "Wait till you're certain."

"Christ Almighty," the Kid said, "they look like P-51s." There was elation in his voice, a release of pressure, and whoops of joy followed his announcement. Indeed they were P-51 *Mustangs,* which the crew did not expect—but the nimble little fighters did them no good.

Griffin tuned in on the "C" channel, reserved for fighter communications, and he heard Lieutenant Colonel Hagstrom who was leading the forward task force twelve minutes ahead of them, yelling in an attempt to reach the 51s—"Crossbow! Crossbow! Do you copy? This is Pistol One calling Crossbow." But the band was manned and Griffin could not hear the response. From the urgent sound of the call, Hagstrom's task force was catching hell and needed help badly.

The way this was supposed to work and the way things actually did work were two different arrangements. The P-51s were assigned to sweep over the bombers in a column of squadrons at two or three minute intervals, giving what was called "corridor support." The tactic was designed to keep the German fighters away, or at least diminish their effectiveness. But after three passes over Sutton's squadron the P-51s vanished. This was a bad sign—it meant that things were unusually hot where Hagstrom's element was, and that Sutton's force would be without fighter escort. The Germans would see this and wait, attacking as soon as the *Forts* passed through the main concentration of shell fire.

The sky filled with angry black bursts. Griffin saw one of the bombers, *The Intruder,* catch a direct hit that ignited the bomb load with a terrific explosion. His mouth went dry and he took a deep nervous breath, sensing the panic of *The Intruder*'s crew. The sky vibrated and waved and a moment later the ship no longer existed. The wings, still joined like two silver blades, left a contorted plume of fiery smoke as they spiraled madly to the earth. The nose section and the bulk of the fuselage disappeared. The biggest piece, the tail assembly, spun slowly down, a huge metal "T" with no aerodynamic value. No one reported parachutes. As Griffin watched he thought of himself, thought of his worst fear: being trapped in the cockpit by centrifugal force, knowing that you are going to crash and being helpless to save yourself. A few moments later he looked down at the spot where *The Intruder* had exploded—tufts of smoke marked the area like a tombstone.

Gibson checked his charts. "There isn't supposed to be flak here," he said to no one in particular over the interphone.

"Tell that to Cook," Griffin said, referring to *The Intruder*'s 26-year-old aircraft commander.

Gibson was correct, found it odd that they were getting shot at from a spot that wasn't in the briefing. Rarely did a heavy disposition of AA guns turn up that hadn't been previously estimated. Gibson came on the interphone again: "Four minutes to the I.P."

The I.P.—the Initial Point—was a pre-determined spot on the ground where a Group's squadrons turned into the target and was usually announced four or five minutes before it was reached.

"All right," Sutton said calmly, "let's get set, this is going to be a real lulu." It was a pilot's intuition talking. The vanishing P-51s, flak where there was no flak reported—all these things made Sutton certain that the mission was about to get very rough.

The Group flew a javelin formation, which was composed of three squadrons—the lead, the high, and the low. Sutton's today was high, a favorite German target because it was particularly vulnerable to overhead attacks.

In March 1944, a new "fanning out" procedure was adopted to accomplish the turn over the I.P. and enabled all three squadrons to turn and then fly the briefed bomb run to the target. As a result, all three squadrons maintained altitude, had enough interval to avoid collision, and flew the same course without having to identify the target individually.

One minute from the I.P. Kid Kiley reported a formation of German fighters sweeping up from below.

TWO

Georg-Peter Eder's *Schwarm* passed through 15,000 feet at full throttle, a crisp tight formation five miles behind the low squadron in Sutton's Group. Eder tightened his shoulder harness, stashed his map, checked his Revi 16B reflector gunsight, then quickly scanned his gun switches making certain they were in the fire mode. He depressed his mike button: "Wait for my command." In less than a minute the *Schwarm* would divide into two flights of two aircraft. Over Eder's shoulders, a mixed group of thirty-five Luftwaffe—Bf-190s and FW-190s—streamed up to meet the *Forts*.

"All right," Sutton said, "let's have some radio chatter, start calling in your sightings." Griffin noted the sureness in Sutton's voice, that tone of confidence which was also reflected in his deep brown eyes. "I want to hear you, gents, let's start talking."

Eder flew the FW-190A-8 model, the latest production Focke-Wulf had built in large numbers—over 1,300 machines were produced in 1944. The big powerful BMW 801D-2 engine was equipped with an MW50 methanol-water boost system that provided 1,700 horsepower for takeoff and 1,440 horsepower at 18,000 feet. The 25-gallon reservoir tank holding the methanol-water was behind Eder's armored seat, sloshing gently as the *Schwarm* knifed toward the B-17s. For all-weather operation, the fighter had a heated armor glass canopy. Normal armament on A-8s were a pair of MGH131 machine guns set above the engine in the fuselage. But Eder's ship, an "assault fighter" was also used by the *Sturmstaffel* or *Rammjager,* and had a pair of MK108s that replaced the outer wing paneled MG151 guns. (At the suggestion of *Major* von Kornatsku, a Luftwaffe officer, volunteers from various units formed *Sturmstaffel I* in which each pilot had signed a declaration vowing that he would not return to base without having destroyed an enemy bomber—even to the point of ramming it as a last resort.)

"Mother of God!" shouted Kiley. "I've got four . . . coming at me . . . closing fast . . . coming straight up."

"All right, get on 'em," said Sutton.

Tutone swung his turret rearward, anxious to meet the enemy.

"Hey, hold the phone. There's about two dozen more coming up behind them," Skolinsky said from the Sperry ball turret that hung beneath *The Beast.* He was in the least-enviable station in the bomber, wrapped fetuslike in a cocoon of glass and steel, severely exposed to German gunfire and flak. If he ever thought about the danger, he frequently told the others, he'd never climb back in.

What happened in the next few minutes no one in *The Beast*—not even Tutone, always eager to meet the enemy, and Rowe, who always anticipated the worst—was quite prepared to face. All of them, when they saw the swarms of sleek fighters, felt an icy lump of fear in their bellies a moment after the shock of surprise had flushed their skin. *The Beast,* their good and true friend, their ship, seemed to have betrayed them, to have taken them into a nightmare—one of the most intense fighter attacks they had encountered.

Squadron after squadron of enemy fighters peeled off after them, their turning, spiraling, twisting streams seeming endlessly accurate. Time seemed to have stopped in favor of the Luftwaffe, to give the German fighter pilots all the opportunity they needed to make their attacks. This was a highly coordinated, well-planned assault, not only between fighters in a flight, but between the flights of fighters as well. Once the fighters started bearing down on *The Beast* they were like a pack of frenzied sharks intent on doing their best—in consecutive swoops—to tear it to pieces before going on to ravage others. The end to all of this was as distant as eternity, and as incomprehensible.

Eder's flights were word coded—his was Sword, the second flight, Hawk. At 20,000 feet, the *Schwarm* was above the flight level of the high squadron and "closing fast," as Kiley had reported a second ago. The plan was that Eder and his wingman, the young and jittery *Oberstleutnant* Egon Ruf, would break right when they reached the rear of the high squadron then go into a split-S maneuver—a 180° rotation about the aircraft's longitudinal axis, followed by a 180° change of heading in the vertical plane. The maneuver would consume distance and take Eder's Sword flight beyond the lead ships in the high squadron, putting them in a position for one of his infamous frontal assaults. Hawk flight would break left ten degrees and then attack from above after an Immelman maneuver—in which the aircraft completes the first half of a loop, rolls over to an upright position, and thus flies back in the opposite direction with a simultaneous gain in altitude. Hawk flight would attack the high squadron from the ten o'clock position, while Eder's flight would make a frontal attack.

"Break!" ordered Eder.

"They're splitting into two flights," Kiley reported.

"Jesus," Griffin mumbled, an impatient, anger-filled sentence. He glanced through his side window and saw the fighters—Eder and Ruf—sweep past less than a hundred yards off the right wing tip. "Right in the middle of the bomb run," Griffin said. "They couldn't have picked a worse time."

Sutton told Griffin to knock it off. "Keep your eyes peeled and call out your sightings."

Rowe reached for the bomb door handle and the bomb bay doors swung open like big clam shells.

Two miles ahead of *The Beast,* Eder and Ruf dropped down to 18,000 feet, the level of Sutton's squadron.

"Two coming straight in," Sutton said.

Rowe glanced up over his aiming panel, surprised at the two specks flying toward him. He grabbed the yoke that controlled the action of the Bendix chin turret and aimed at Ruf's ship, speeding toward him now at more than 300 miles an hour. The bombardier's compartment, shared with the navigator, was capped at the nose by a glass blister with only an inverted U-shaped frame. The blister on earlier models was framed into ten glass sections; but this model, the B-17G, had frameless nose-glazing that gave the bombardier a clearer field of vision.

Tutone responded to Sutton's call and swung his Sperry turret around, face forward, and picked up Eder and Ruf winging in. "Bastards, and I have a date tonight," he grumbled with mock anger. He aimed at the fighter on the left, *Oberstleutnant* Egon Ruf, quickly making certain of the range and deflection, then waited one more second to be sure.

At that moment Sword flight did not know that four .50-caliber machine guns were trained on Ruf's Focke-Wulf. Nor did they know that in less than three seconds Ruf's ship would take over forty hits from the powerful guns. On Eder's order, they activated the MW50 system injecting the methanol-water into the super-chargers and thus provided a performance boost that kicked in 1,440 horsepower. Speed was essential. Eder knew that a fast moving ship that danced and swayed in the air "like a nervous bird," would make an extremely difficult target for the American gunners. Ruf had been instructed to use his rudder pedals, to juke his ship through the air, to slip and slide like a fast moving crab while keeping the big bomber framed in his Revi—no simple task. And the key was to press the attack until the last possible second, guns blazing through the duration, and then to turn away just before ramming the bomber. It took courage, determination, and an uncanny ability to concentrate, to block everything else from one's head.

Eder had *The Beast* framed on his reflector gunsight, adjusting the glare with a small black knob. His ship felt light, nimble, beautifully balanced like an expensive sports car, and the powerful BMW engine sang with an even *basso* roar. He focused hard on his target as he always did, saw the top turret and the chin turret on *The Beast* rolling around ominously.

"They are turning at us . . . they have us spotted," he radioed to Ruf, who wanted to wrench his aircraft away. This was his first head-on attack and his body was filled with a sharp penetrating fear. How could anyone do this—how could you charge head-on into the enemy's guns so brazenly, without regard for your own life? Was Eder truly crazy?

This was something for fools, Ruf thought, knowing that in less than a second the muzzles from the American bomber would flare with gun fire, that tracers would be streaming out toward him, that the gunners would do their best to blow him out of the sky. He thought of his mother, how he wanted to see her again; he imagined her handing his snapshot to friends, an ambivalent act, he was sure. Yes, she was proud that Egon was a fighter pilot for the Reich; but she had such a fear, such a loathing for this war and what it could do to her. Today, the young *Oberstleutnant* was wearing a new gray-flannel blouse, a gift from his mother. Shorter than the service tunic, it had one row of hidden plastic buttons with slanted outside pockets. The silver Luftwaffe eagle was hand-embroidered by Herr Baer, the village tailor. The fresh silver bullion collar patches glinted sharply in the brilliant light, their reflection beaming back into Ruf's pale blue eyes off the thick windscreen near the Revi gunsight. Yes, the *Oberst-*

leutnant wished to turn away, sharply, and leave this place forever; but because of the pressure of his flight leader, the famous Eder, Ruf pressed on. He gripped the control stick with a sweaty glove until his knuckles turned a scared pink. Thinking of his mother, his thumb felt for the firing button.

"Fire!" shouted Eder.

The word stung Ruf's ears through his headset but he obeyed.

Eder's Focke-Wulf shuttered like a jackhammer, the 20mm cannons roared and spent shell casings spewed out from the cartridge shuts under the wings, little brass trinkets glimmering gold in the clear light.

Tutone saw the muzzles flash on the FW-190s, saw the tracers bending toward *The Beast.* Had he known what happened, the uncanny miracle that just took place, he would have made a special prayer to the Blessed Virgin Mary. Eder's first burst was on target but he had fired too soon and the tracers fell, missing the nose of *The Beast* by seven inches. If Eder had waited another fifteenth of a second the shells would have penetrated the cockpit and Tutone's turret. The trajectory carried the rounds toward another ship, *Roselle's Raiders,* flying below and behind *The Beast.*

Each cannon in the Focke-Wulf's wing pods fired at the rate of 420 pounds per minute. Every third shell was thin-cased containing 19.5 grams of Hexogen Al high-explosive filling, an armor-piercing shell with a reinforced tip and an incendiary that burned at a temperature of approximately 2,500 degrees centigrade for nearly one second. Theoretically, fifteen of these would deal a lethal blow. The first slammed through the bombardier's glass blister in *Roselle's*

Raiders, which shattered inward from the velocity of the slipstream like fine-grained snow. The shock-force was so terrific that the bombardier actually had no idea what happened. The glass fragments and wind combined into an abrasive tearing the skin from his face like coarse jelly. He had no time to gasp, to scream, to feel pain. The round missed his chin by an inch but exploded on contact with one of the portable oxygen tanks on the upper right-hand side of the compartment, bursting the tank and breaking open a four-foot gash in the fuselage. The contents hydrated into a cloud of white mist. One-twentieth of a second later the second shell slammed through the cockpit, exploding under the pilot's feet. Two seconds after the bang diminished the pilot thought the instrument panel had fallen and caused the clatter. When he looked down he saw that his feet were missing—in the interior at 100 miles an hour like a cannon ball gone haywire.

Seconds before this, a dozen of Eder's rounds, through pure chance, passed through the front wing spar terminal. Although these dozen rounds were destructive, the final killing blow was accomplished when a singular H.E. shell sparked a fire in the left inboard wing tank. One and a half minutes later the wing, mated to the fuselage with loving care at Boeing's California plant, crumpled with an hysterical shriek. The inboard wing panel, mated to the outboard wing panel by a set of thirteen taper pins, melted like sliced cheese on a hot gridle. While this happened the turret gunner, dazed and vomiting, successfully made his way to the opened bomb bay doors and jumped. But without his parachute.

The pilot of *Roselle's Raiders* could not hold her

level. Oh God, dear God, the awful pain in his legs! Dropping through the air like a toy airplane, the pilot looked out and saw the wing just as it folded, motioning over the fuselage as if to bid the mother ship a last farewell before it disappeared over the shattered turret. *I'm going to die,* the pilot thought, and three and a half minutes later, still trying desperately to dislodge himself from his harness, he hit the earth.

Rowe fired his guns. The deafening roar slammed through the compartment in huge explosive bangs. "I got one! I got one!" he screamed. But his claim was premature; his tracers had streaked two feet above Ruf's canopy. In the next instant, Rowe corrected his aim by a hair and the rounds pierced the nose of Ruf's FW-190.

Twenty-two shells hit the German fighter. Some glanced and ricocheted, sparking white as they smacked the painted skin. Ruf felt a bang. His ship stuttered and side-slipped. A second later, there was a mild explosion, like a barbell hitting a steel floor. The aircraft stammered and Ruf, stunned, checked his throttle setting and noted that it hadn't moved. "What the—" After flying this crazy head-on attack for eight seconds the *Oberstleutnant* could not comprehend why his ship was slowing. If he could step out and open the cowling around the engine he would not have been surprised.

Because of early cooling problems the BMW engine had to be cooled by a ten-bladed fan that spun just behind the propeller spinner. Two rounds from Rowe's turret guns, after crashing through the spinning prop and nicking the outer edges on two of the blades, passed into this speeding fan. The 5mm fixed-nose ring armor on the leading edge of the engine cowling was there to protect the ten-gallon oil tanks. Actually there were two crescent-shaped tanks in the nose section at the top half of the cowling forward of the 2-bank BMW motor. When the shells passed through the prop they had a deceleration rate of 800 times the force of gravity and the fan disintegrated. The explosive force sent variously shaped chunks of red hot steel upward through the oil tanks, and the hot thick brown viscous fluid streaked over the bulletproof windscreen Ruf was trying to see through. This had an alarming effect on the young pilot, though not approaching the threshold of panic. Already choking slightly from the sting of gunsmoke pouring into his cockpit from the burning oil that splashed across the engine, Ruf sensed a release of acid from his stomach into the back of his mouth and began to gag.

Rowe's next two-second burst did the trick. Shells raked Ruf's fighter along the belly from nose to tail, the impact of the fourteen shells easily visible, each sparking and tearing through the alloy skin marked by puffs of dust and atomized paint. At 2,450 RPM, and after attaining a true airspeed of 375 miles an hour, the fighter now seemed to have flown into a cloud of steel. Some of the rounds passed harmlessly through the airframe—one bent a fish plate on the outside near the tailplane mainspar. The fifth round got lucky and came through the cockpit floor, nicking Ruf's thigh and smashing through the throttle quadrant. This was the *Kommandgerat,* or "brain box," part of a finely built, complex unit that measured 16 x 16 x 12 and was located just ahead of the engine mount ring. When the pilot moved the throttle lever forward this hydraulic-electric unit automatically adjusted fuel flow, fuel mixture, propeller pitch setting and ignition—and at the proper altitude this little jewel cut in the second stage of the supercharger. But if the pilot desired to make a prop pitch change without altering the setting, he did so manually by pushing a rocking lever switch set in the throttle. But now the device was shattered into hundreds of pieces.

"Hell!" *Release firing button, stick back, gain altitude.* Confused, panic-filled, the *Oberstleutnant* with the new flying blouse and shiny Luftwaffe eagle reached down for the emergency handle located near the canopy crank. Ruf was bailing out.

"I got 'em! I got 'em!" Rowe yelled.

Eder turned back into the attack using strong left rudder to swing the nose around and scanned the sky and saw Ruf's ship falling, streaming ribbons of pink flame.

Sutton looked at the clock on the instrument panel. It was ten twenty-four, they were supposed to have been ten minutes west of Pontoise completely rejoined and flying toward England. "Some son of a bitch in Wing had a pencil up his ass sideways when he planned this one," Sutton said into the interphone. The Group was all over the sky and the Germans came back, attacking stragglers, using line-abreast and javelin formations. There were concentrated attacks and some freelancers working the shambles that was now the Group. Once one spotted a weakness others would join in and probe and peck like a pack of wolves. They were sharp today, hitting and running, and only after their mags were empty did they disappear and head for home and a hot

37

meal and game of cards.

The 45th Bombardment Group lost ten ships that day and the time back to England seemed interminable. Sutton was unusually silent, steaming because he felt Griffin hadn't done his job effectively—spotting and calling out attacks, coordinating the ranges of fire among *The Beast*'s gunners. Tutone, who was usually glib and peppy, was so quiet Sutton called him on the interphone to see if he was all right.

The Beast dropped into the landing circle and, as everyone expected, several red flares shot off from the bombers: wounded or dead aboard; make way for an emergency landing; get the old meat wagons out. They circled around, waiting their turn, watching the field, the ambulances pulling up to the landed ships then streaking toward the medical building.

"Sons of bitches at Wing," Sutton said. "All right, let's get it down," he told Griffin.

Griffin watched the instruments, the pressure and the temperatures. He dropped the landing gear and saw the green signal light under the tachs flash on, checked to be sure the tail wheel was down and locked, made certain the cowl-flap valves were locked. Then he began calling out the decreasing airspeed for Sutton. In between he called back and made sure Skolinsky had set the ball turret with the guns horizontal and pointing to the rear.

"One forty-six . . . one forty-four . . . one-forty. . . ."

"Flaps," Sutton ordered and Griffin lowered them.

Gently, Sutton adjusted the trim tabs while Griffin kept calling out the airspeed. When the tail wheel came down Griffin raised the flaps and then the brakes screeched then quieted as the ship rolled to taxiing speed. Tutone unstrapped himself and dropped through the forward hatch and waved Sutton in.

Then Tutone stood there, stiff and bow-legged, watched the props jerk to a halt, smelled the rich odor of burnt gas—the unmistakable odor of a B-17 after combat. Less than a hundred yards away, Captain Chrisp's ship, *This Is It!*, taxied to a halt. Before the engines stopped a meat wagon came to a screeching halt near the rear door of the aircraft. Three attendants ran to the plane carrying a stretcher.

Tutone shook his head, a gesture of sadness. He turned away, pulled out a pack of beaten Lucky Strikes and tried to think of something else—his date tonight in London with Charlotte, the stocky swimmer who loved classical music. The only reason for the stretcher was to carry out the belly gunner's remains.

This Is It!'s belly turret was a mass of twisted, burnt metal split open by a direct hit. What remained of the gunner was a gruesome sight. The ambulance attendants were inside and worked quickly with hammers and wire cutters before they could drag away the lower portion, leaving a trail as they tugged away. Outside, a member of the medical department stood by with a hose. The tail gunner approached to lend a hand but when he looked at the horror he screamed and stumbled through the rear door, dazed. Only a few hours ago his friend had been alive; but now all his dreams, every bad joke he'd heard or told, every emotion he ever had, was a thick smear across a cold metal runway on the floor of a damaged B-17.

Without looking, Tutone knew what was going on. He lit a cigarette and waited for his crew to empty out of *The Beast*.

Debriefing took forty-five minutes but Sutton and Tutone and the rest of the crew had to stand around the Red Cross truck for half an hour drinking coffee, waiting their turn in silence. There was a lot of activity to report today.

An hour later Tutone picked up a telephone and called London. Charlotte's voice was soft and bright, lacked the pain heard in so many voices today. It was a sweet voice and the sound of it, the accent and expectation ringing with it as Charlotte spoke, took Benny Tutone away from the madness of Bassingbourn, away from his nightmares.

"How are you," Charlotte asked, after a slight giggle.

"I like you," Tutone said.

"Why?"

"You don't make me nervous."

THREE

Sutton entered Colonel Branch Parker's office.

"Please, have a seat," Parker said curtly, after returning Sutton's crisp salute.

The office was a mixture of English and American furniture purchased or "borrowed" by Sergeant Litton. It had a peculiar, distinctive odor—a mustiness mixed with the scent of a sweet aftershave or a cheap perfume, and the lingering smell of stale cigarettes and burnt pipe tobacco. The oak desk was bought from an insurance firm in London and the obsequious Litton sent off to haul it back via Army truck. A sofa with big round arms shone leather-green in the dull light against a freshly painted wall.

Parker lounged in a tall desk chair that rocked, an item acquired from an auction of furniture from a defunct Chicago advertising firm. Parker was the 45th Bombardment Group's commanding officer—referred to unaffectionately as "Old Irontail." But there was nothing old about the ambitious 39-year-old career officer, a wily calculating Midwesterner determined to make brigadier general before his fortieth birthday.

Sutton disliked Parker and the feeling was subtly but distinctly returned. Parker's rank and his office were respected; but it was the man himself that Sutton despised.

Sutton took a chair in front of Parker's desk, a montage of the man's thus-far successful career: a couple of West Point photos with fellow cadets, a pose shaking hands with Generals Eisenhower and Eaker, a hole-in-one golf ball perched atop a small wooden base carved with the word *Hooray!,* that sort of thing.

"Captain," Parker said, glancing through steel-rimmed eyeglasses that magnified his small fishy eyes, "you seem to have a penchant for finding trouble wherever you go." The drawl was thicker when he was annoyed, as if he had a mouthful of marbles.

"How so?" asked Sutton.

"I'm speaking about the flak, Captain. I'm just making a general statement."

There was a natural dislike between these two men, a gloom that draped over them when they were together, that had enveloped them the first moment they met.

Parker—ever so careful to guard and plan each career move, as a chessman in a tournament—had asked Wing for Sutton to lead the top secret Sperrle mission. Parker wanted Sutton, his qualifications: crop duster and stunt flyer before the war. Parker had smelled success, chased after it like a hungry fox pursuing the rabbit of ambition. If the mission would succeed so would Parker, and he was correct. Sutton was transferred (involuntarily) from another Group. Afterward, a citation was slipped into Parker's 66-1 personnel file, and General Eaker called and followed up with a small sterling silver cigarette case from Tiffany's.

There were only two men in the Group that Parker respected: Captain Chrisp, who admired Parker's cunning, calculating way since it resembled his own; and Roger Griffin, Sutton's new copilot, who, in 1938, had demonstrated the dreaded outside loop to the world in a Griffin Aircraft Company-built RG-4 *Aerohound.* "My boy, Griff," Parker told some starstruck officers at Wing, "can do anything." Both men, unlike Sutton, could promote old Irontail in their own matchless ways. While Chrisp's Army Air Force father was on the Pentagon board that promoted colonels to brigadier general, Griffin was a young celebrity aviator, heir to the Griffin Aircraft Corporation in upstate New York, and second-place winner of the 1937 Thompson Trophy Air Race. Sutton's father owned a dirt airstrip, also in New York and not far from the Griffin factory. When Griffin left for England, his father deposited ten-thousand dollars in his checking account "to show those Limeys what cloth the Griffins are cut from." The day Sutton left, his father stuck an old Zippo lighter in his son's hand, a gift from his wife months before she died. "Your asshole's a little punchy, so you're going to need this more than me," Sutton's father said when they left each other at the train station.

Before a crowd of thousands, including Ernst Udet, the World War I flying ace and head of the Luftwaffe's Technical Department, Roger completed the dreaded

43

outside loop on May 8th, 1938. To achieve the outside loop, the pilot flies toward the top of an imaginary wheel, pushes forward on the control column, noses over, scribes a circle around the outside of the wheel, then flies out level again from the top at the point of entry. The feat required an airplane that could withstand the "G" forces applied to the airframe during the maneuver; but an untested *Aerohound* and a false sense of courage were all Roger Boy had had. What really drove Roger was his father, a boisterous, flamboyant, hard-drinking businessman. Enter Jim Sutton.

Three days before Rog's ascension into Aerial Heaven, two doublebreasted-suit types drove over from Poughkeepsie in a maroon Chevvy and offered Sutton $10,000 in cash to give the loop a shot in the old *'Hound*. Sutton had already flown the loop in an oil-smeared *Travel Air 4000K* with a busted fuel gauge and control lines lousy with too much play—unknown to the world, so the offer was a solid shot at copping ten grand without much effort. And the Suttons certainly needed the dough.

"If you agree," one of the men told Jim Sutton, "you'll have to sign a waiver and a sworn statement that you won't tell anyone that Griffin Aircraft owns the *Aerohound*. After you sign, you get in the plane, hit the loop, and when you land you get the dough."

"What if I'm killed?" asked Sutton, looking for assurances that his father would get the money. His father owned the airstrip. After all, the taxman and the bank were a short distance away from tomorrow and the chances of losing the airstrip were here and now. Despite a protest from Sutton's father, the suits told

Jim either way the money was his. The next day Sutton gave them two perfect loops and forgot the matter. Until three weeks ago when Roger, announced to the world as the newest member of the 45th Bombardment Group by Parker, arrived at Bassingbourn. Since then, Sutton had kept his promise. No one—except the doublebreasted suits and Griffin's father—knew he had flown the loop. Roger got the credit and Parker thought that indeed he had a boy wonder within his ranks.

"Now," Parker said, tapping an ash into a brass ashtray, "Captain Chrisp said things were unusually hot before you hit the I.P."

"I don't doubt that. His belly gunner was killed. Colonel, you never call me in here for simple chit-chat, so why not just get to the point."

"That *is* the point, Captain." Parker's eyelids twitched. "As you know, Major Marks neglected to mention the possibility of flak between Pontoise and Paris—nothing neglectful on his part, I can assure you. But we didn't expect the mission to go as badly as it did. Did you have lunch?"

Sutton shook his head. "Colonel, I've got a few things to do, why don't we just get on with this."

Parker owned a big dog named Rag Tag, a German shepherd. Everyone disliked the dog—one of those big animals that appeared resentful with big sloppy lips and large pointy teeth, eyes that twitched occasionally like Parker's. In a corner, behind Sutton, the dog stood and traipsed slowly toward Parker, growling once at Sutton's boots. Parker leaned back in his chair and folded his arms, then he reached down and patted Rag Tag's big furry head.

"I've tried," he said to Sutton, "to get along with you, Captain. But it seems you have a natural disrespect, a dislike for superiors." Parker shot away from his chair and leaned over the edge of his desk. "I've often said, Captain, that you march to a different drummer. Perhaps that's what it takes for you to get out of your rack each morning and face the day—the fact that you are an excellent airman, a terrific pilot. But why, for God's sake, can't you be a little more cooperative?"

Sutton stood and looked down at Parker. "Colonel, about a month ago you needed someone—namely me—to fly your Sperrle mission. At that time I told you that I didn't want to fly for you, that I didn't admire your ambition, nor the way you treated your men. Since that time I've come to realize that I was correct in feeling that way. So, instead of discussing lunch, why don't you just get on with the point of this meeting?"

Parker laughed. "The best defense is a good offense, I can see that plainly. Turn the tables on your commanding officer. Okay, Captain, I'll worry about my ambition and you worry about not getting your peter stuck in a prop blade. Because if you keep this up you'll be heading for a court-martial."

"I doubt it, Colonel."

"Why's that?"

"Because you need me."

Parker's knuckles were white. Sutton was correct— if anything important came up and Parker needed someone with special qualifications, Sutton could accomplish the task.

Along the flightline the maintenance crews were combing through their *Fortresses,* fixing, patching, replacing, topping off the tanks. Sergeant Holden, *The*

Beast's sullen-faced but deft crew chief, fired up the Number 1 engine and it coughed and sputtered. Sutton heard its distinctive beat, a father familiar with the cry of his own baby. The engine hummed in the midrange for a few seconds, screaming, Holden playing with the throttle setting, checking the gauges, temperatures, the cowl flaps; then he settled it down into idle and left it fixed there for a while, probably not satisfied. Holden listened to it through the seat of his greasy coveralls, where, Sutton was certain, all the sensitivity in Holden's mechanic's body was concentrated.

Sutton watched *The Beast* in the distance over Parker's bird-like shoulder, not watching the face of the man—the screwy annoyance that washed over him when things didn't blend the way he imagined they should, when he couldn't get his way—and he thought of Holden and the crew of *The Beast*. Initially they were a bag of misfits thrust on him by Parker for the Sperrle mission. But they had come together—except for the star-studded Griffin. Performers they were, wearing their pride silently for their ship, a real "peacheroo" as Tutone called it. So if Sutton had ever wanted to abandon this bunch, the feeling was past tense. And in the end that merely represented a beginning, and more often than not that was the most difficult task—getting together and starting. The way the crew behaved initially was not as important as how Sutton would shape their potential. He was lucky he had them, and for that he was deeply grateful.

"So?" Sutton looked at Parker and waited.

The Colonel put the sheet down, pressed it flat on the blotter, looked up and said: "I have another mission for you and your crew—an important one."

"Aren't they all?"

"I had Marks in here a while ago," Parker said, some of the blood returning to his narrow face. "We agreed that we need you to fly a photographic pass over the Pontoise area to ascertain just what the damned Germans are guarding there and to determine the intensity of the flak. We have more raids in that area in the next few weeks so it would—"

Sutton stood. "Why me? Why do you always pick me for these bastard missions? What's Chrisp doing, got a date with the Princesses? I thought he was swell enough to handle anything."

"Captain Chrisp does not have your low-level experience."

"Then get one of the boys from Colonel Hopper's Recon Group, they're specialists at this."

"They're working overtime on something else. Look, I've volunteered you, Captain. And besides, the top brass at Wing have already concurred. They like you, your work, what you did on the Sperrle mission. So, you're down on the boards for this one. Case closed."

"Swell—I do such a great job that I get picked for all the dangerous missions."

"They're all dangerous, Captain."

"Some are a little nastier than others, Colonel."

Rag Tag opened a sleepy eye and looked over his nose at Parker and sniffed the air.

Sutton sat again, looked dejected, stubbed out his cigarette. "Okay, let's hear it."

Parker opened the folder on his blotter and quickly ran one of his spidery fingers across the typewritten page that set forth permission for his verbal request: *I'll have one of my boys, Jim Sutton, go in and take pictures of that area the way a bomber pilot would like to see them.* So, someone at Wing, a general, a colonel, sensed initiative, knew they were shorthanded, and sent down the official order:

PNT OIBMP OIKHI V NR 109 O-P
FROM GRV 13422 MAY 1944
TO OIBMP
OIKHI
SECRET QQX BT D-60, 514
REQUEST THAT YOU FURNISH THIS HEADQUARTERS IMMEDIATELY WITH A PHOTO INTERPRETATION OF THE PONTOISE AREA. SUCCESS OF MISSION WILL DETERMINE DECISION FOR ATTACKING THIS AREA ON 24 MAY 1944.

PERMISSION GRANTED TO UTILIZE SUTTON, JAMES L.,

CAPTAIN, USAAF.

ET 1345B MAY 44
EJY   K
AS FOR R
ZT

Parker placed the directive down with reverence, smiled to himself, some of his elation seeping through his pores and those strange eyes of his, like a child who'd just snatched a lollipop and gotten away with it. But that was Parker's way—every achievement, every inch gained, added toward attaining the star. "Another star," he would say to his family, "another star, the family needs another star." Parker's father had been a general, and his uncle, too. Fine, bold West Point grads, both of them, who had distinguished themselves in God knows how many wars and battles. Combat tested, combat proven. The real McCoy. Courageous men who'd forged a rough path for old Branch, which was his mother's family name. The Branches were Connecticut Yankees, the Parkers land-owning Virginia gentry that established their military roots in the Civil War. "Hell, that wasn't the Civil War," Parker would say when cocktailing with friends, "that was the war of Northern aggression." When fishing, feet up on the transom of the boat, casting his dreams with the same verve as the fly rod, Parker would see himself bestowed with the rank, *the star,* of brigadier general. It was all he dreamed about; but unlike his battle-marred ancestors, Parker's wars were desk-fought, his trenches hallways, his parapets desks. Because underneath it all, under the glimmer of insignia, under the voice of battle, Parker feared combat more than the fear of failure.

Sutton shifted his weight and checked his watch. In less than an hour, Arianne would be at the gate waiting for him. So now he wanted all the particulars, when they'd fly, was there a practice run, would he use the same crew. . . .

Parker took five minutes to unravel the details, pacing back and forth behind his big desk, moving with nervous energy, hands clasped behind his back like a long slim bird. Sometimes he would stop and peer through the window, checking the sky, the crews in the distance; and when he did this he would become momentarily lost in thought and have to ask Sutton where he left off.

"The mission," Parker said in summation, "is set for the day after tomorrow. The practice run will be here in England tomorrow morning at 0700, and you will be using your own crew. By the way," Parker said, sitting again, careful not to wake the sleeping Rag Tag, "you'll be flying a different ship for this mission."

A short moment later the meeting ended as sullenly as it had begun. Parker slumped back into the pose he'd assumed when Sutton entered, and Sutton saluted with the same punch he mustered when he walked into this dreary place with its mishmash of borrowed and stolen furniture.

FOUR

"All right, I was born in Brooklyn, New York," Tutone said to Charlotte in the dark. "New York City never sleeps. And they don't roll the damned sidewalks up after the birds go off to sleep, and you can get something to eat at two or three in the morning, just like that. People from Manhattan, the real high-hats, they think Brooklyn stinks, but what the hell do they know. They live on an island they stole from a bunch of Indians. Brooklyn, my home town. I love the damned place.

"My family never had any real dough, and my father drives a hack, that's a taxi, which is what I'll probably do when the war's over.

"And you want to know something? My old man's my hero. I mean, I love the guy. He's done a lot for me just by being my pal. He's done a little bit of everything and not much of anything—sort of this and that, that's what kind of guy he is: a dock worker, a truck driver, lots of things. His name is Benito, Benny, like me, and my mother, whenever she called us, we got confused. So now she says, Big Benny—that's my father—and little Benny—that's me. My mother says, 'Benny, you were made for beauty, not speed.' She almost died when I said I was thinking about trying out for football. 'You won't do well at it,' she said. My mother is never wrong, believe me.

"I graduated third in my class. I had to bust my rear end to get grades like that. Richie Sorentino was second, and some other guy named Bruce Wesley, a real high-hat, was first, and neither one of those bastards had to crack a book. Me, I had to study all the time. Richie Sorentino is a fighter pilot in the Navy and they say he's doing great, that he could make admiral. I'm glad for him. And Wesley has a desk job in the Pentagon. A code cracker. What the hell, I wish him the Pentagon. A code cracker. What the hell, I wish him good luck, too. Come to think of it, I wish everybody good luck.

"What I really like is music. Swing, big band, Miller, Dorsey, and that kid, Frank Sinatra. Even the classical stuff you have on the Victrola is swell. What's that you have on there—Chopin? Hah! See, I know my music.

"I started playing the drums when I was thirteen. I got hooked on Gene Krupa when I saw him at the Metropole. That's a joint in Manhattan. Manhattan is like twelve Londons, no offense intended. Manhattan is a swell place. Krupa was there—I can still see him swingin', and the place was jumpin' and I said, God, that's what I have to do, I have to play those things just like that and move my hands that fast. Sometimes I think that's what I'll do when the war's over, drive a cab and play the drums and make some dough. I want to do a lot of things when the war's over. . . .

"Am I good?

"Hah! You've got to be jiving me! Of course I'm good.

"I have this friend, name's Johnny Tessa, a piano player with long slim fingers. We used to gig together, that means play the same dates, okay, just so you know the term from now on. Tess, that's what we call him, is in the Pacific playing on a .30-caliber Browning machine gun. He always wanted to see the Pacific, being from Brooklyn and all. Gee, I wonder if Tess is doing all right out there?

"Tess and I, we had a gig out in Queens, that's a borough in New York City— Hey, I wonder if they named it after your Queen? After, we drove over to LaGuardia Field. Tess, he says to me, 'Hey, Benzo'— that's what he calls me—'they got a bomber here, a real B-17.' So, we walked over and I looked and talked with one of the crewmen, the turret gunner. That's what did it for me. Eight months later, the war breaks out and I know instantly what I want to do, I want to jump into a 17 like that guy I spoke with and be a gunner. You know something, it's almost like playing the drums. Believe me, it really is. Are you sleeping or what?

"Some people say I talk too much. I get sore when I hear that because I'm just trying to make an effort. I mean, did you ever hear that spot in a conversation where there isn't any noise, no talk. God, that's awful. You don't know what to do with your hands.

"I don't like to do anything to hurt anyone. Pollyanna the glad guy, that's Benny for you.

"How would I describe myself?

55

"Well, easy going. I don't expect too much so when I get a little something, I'm grateful. I guess I'm generous, I'm sentimental and I hate that because . . . Jesus! I never told this to anyone, Charlotte, but sometimes I cry. When Dick Page died I cried for two days, but only when I was alone. I'm not weird or anything. I'm just easygoing, straight and level.

"Let's see now, what else—

"I really don't mind the war—can you believe that? I mean, I feel I'm doing something, doing my part. Jakey, a pal of mine in Brooklyn, he's flat-footed and 4-F, he says he envies me. Imagine that! Somebody envies me, Benny Tutone. Jakey says, 'You're doing a job for America and when it's over America will do a job for you.' I wonder what the hell he means. I mean . . . I wonder if America will. . . .

"Listen, the other thing is my boss, Jim Sutton. Christ, I love the guy. Hey, wait, I'm not queer or anything, so don't worry. Sutton's a real swell guy. You know, the Rhett Butler type. 'Frankly my dear, I don't give a damn'—that's the boss for ya. A good Joe, none of that *hoi polloi* stuff. A while ago he had to straighten the crew out and he put it on the line hard, not caring what we thought about him, just doing the right thing. You know, I can say to him, 'Hey, boss!' I don't have to say, 'Hey, Captain, sir!' That means a lot, it really does.

"I wonder if I left anything out. Well, I guess I did, but what the hell, I'm tired, too.

"Do you understand all this—?"

Tutone had an odd feeling there in the dark that maybe Charlotte didn't care, that he was just rambling, that there was such a gap between their nationalities that she couldn't comprehend a word he just said. Or

56

that he didn't reveal himself as much as he wanted to.

There never seemed to be enough time.

But what else could he explain? There really was so much. There was so much he wanted to share with Charlotte.

"Did you hear what I was saying?"

Charlotte nodded her chin on Tutone's chest, a small comforting sensation. And then she said, *Yes, I heard every word and I loved listening to you.* She held him, brought him closer to her heart.

Tutone didn't tell Charlotte everything. No. There in the dark he could not have told her about his fears, which he wanted so desperately to share with someone, with her. Because that would just make her sad.

Sutton.

There was so much to say about him.

He wasn't any more disillusioned than the other young fliers. Beneath his sober honesty and sense of purpose there was, for that time, a belief in some of America's more solid foundations: *Time,* a lazy Sunday afternoon, the New York Yankees, *Life, Colliers,* a good steak dinner, a chance some day to earn enough dough to take a cruise to the Caribbean. There was very little of the idealism, though, that popped off the Coca Cola ads in *National Geographic.* No, none of that stuff for the boss. If he dreamed, they were dreams of reality and reasonable choice, things based on his knowledge of who he was, what his limits were. He was a solid guy, purely American, filled with just as much fear as the rest, possessing what was then commonly known as *a rage to live.* Survival was achieved through increments, inches, not overwhelming goals that reached disproportionately out into an unknown future: *completing this takeoff, getting through this flak, completing this raid, getting the crew to work together just once more.* Sutton was bothered of course like the rest of them with the prospects of living, the odds, his chances for survival, and he knew the more you went up the greater the chance was you'd never come back down. But maybe that wasn't true either. It was really fate and that was that. Because plenty of fliers were killed on their first raids, while others lived through a couple of dozen without a scratch.

And there was his Stateside girl, Allison, who'd written one stinking letter in the past six weeks. How could she do that? Sutton wondered. He could hear her now, moaning about gas rationing, having to make sacrifices on the home front, *and that bastard Roosevelt, we all wonder if he knows what he's doing.* Rough life. Big house in New Jersey, short hop to the beach, an apartment in Manhattan. If Sutton was loyal to her it was loyalty through routine, not dedication. But God, she had the longest most perfect gams and firmest rear end this side of the Mississippi. And those breasts! If Sutton thought about Allison too long it would drive him mad. Because here he was fighting this damned war, removed from the political rhetoric of the politicians while Allison cruised back and forth to Atlantic City in her big Buick enjoying the comfort of her family's money. Oh, no, Sutton didn't believe he was out there fighting gallantly for a cause, to rid the world of the Nazi threat; it wasn't that—it was just that Allison didn't seem to give a toot for him anymore.

The sun's lemon-yellow rays had dissolved a couple of hours ago and now Sutton was sitting in Arianne's oak-paneled living room—that big comfortable empty place left to her by her late husband, a pilot killed in the Battle of Britain. Clipped bushes and manicured lawns rolled away from the square-cut stones that formed a baronial mansion; the whole set-up left you impressed with its wealth and charm.

Arianne came into the room, haughty, listless, tossing her silky champagne-colored hair over her shoulders, looking proud but troubled: a boyish figure with ice-blue eyes filled with intelligence. While she moved from one end of the room toward Sutton he recalled their first time upstairs in the bedroom during a thunderstorm that matched the ferocity and vigor of their lovemaking. But now his mind lingered on variations, long gentle caresses, new explorations, the things you never had time to realize the first time. They had done it with such strength, such depth and verve, that it frightened both of them—particularly Sutton. He wondered about the meaning of their act. Was it love, was Arianne in love with him, was it some golden symbol that beckoned toward something fresh, that deserved pursuit? Or were they merely physically attracted to each other, lonely people coming together in bed on a black stormy night?

Oh, the movement of her, the lines of her slim graceful figure as she neared the coffee table; it made him forget Allison. The hell with her. Who needed her damned letters, minor statements of her boredom?

Arianne put down a silver tray with two champagne glasses and a magnum of Moet. As she poured, neat fingers holding the glasses gently, Sutton asked about

59

her late husband, an RAF *Spitfire* pilot.

Arianne appeared surprised, lifted her beautiful head an inch.

"What's to say?" she wondered obliquely.

The glasses were filled and Arianne handed Sutton one and said with a flat tone, "The marriage was partially arranged. Our families had been gently insisting that we meet at first. Then after a while there were outings together, that sort of thing. He was a very strong man, I mean, strong-willed, confident." She sipped and looked into Sutton's brown eyes. "Like you," she added without wavering her stare, smiling at him.

"Like me? God!"

"Yes, that same sureness, that same gentleness and understanding."

Sutton laughed, threw back his head, then took the glass of champagne Arianne handed him. "Tell that to my crew."

"They wouldn't understand," Arianne said, sitting on the couch next to Sutton.

Time passed too quickly here, while time in the air over the target seemed an eternity. And there was so much more to discover here. Sutton had heard someone say that you could judge a man by the woman he kept company with. So what was the meaning of this, what was there about himself that he could discover through Arianne?

Suddenly Arianne put her glass down and kissed him. An impulse of the heart, a yearning of the moment that she could not allow to pass. And what was the meaning of *that?* he wondered.

Allison wasn't this way. Allison was American and

60

American girls didn't have this charm, this alluring coyness—they were much more blunt, straight forward.

"Tell me," Arianne said, tilting her head after they'd kissed, "what do you love about your country?"

Sutton thought for a moment—not about the question, but about Arianne. . . .

She had come into his life only a very short time ago, and they had tried to create something. And since then, once in a while, she had smiled at his nostalgic ways. He had never made Arianne think twice about how he felt because, despite him, she always knew who he was and what he could be. Her loneliness had been filled by this quiet American with the crooked smile and brown eyes. Sentimental fools, both of them. But love comes and goes, forced upon us by circumstances and the illusions we create—the momentary images we extend to one another. Arianne had a place in his life: but was it a place to be reached, or had they already left it in the drumming of a thunderstorm a short time ago? What a fool wants to see he sees, and only the wiseman has the power to reason away the illusions that seem to be.

"Well?"

"Well what?" asked Sutton.

"You were away for a while."

"Yes, I was thinking."

"Thinking about home, about America?"

"Natch," he said, lying. Because no matter how much you care for someone, no matter how much you entrust them with those things you keep hidden, there are some things that you can never share. It is the way we are and we can never change that.

Arianne asked softly, leaning over toward Sutton,

"How do you feel?"

"Sentimental," Sutton told her.

Arianne nodded, and then she said, "Tell me what you love about America. Have you seen most of your country?"

This was one of the reasons Sutton cared for Arianne: her genuine concern. She made an effort to reach out, to show willingly how understanding she was. Sutton was alone here and Arianne knew his lament better than anyone: she experienced it every night. So it would have been easier for her to talk about herself, her own fears and pain and loneliness, what she expected of the future. But she didn't; instead, she reached out. And for a moment Sutton could have let himself go similiarly and expressed his feelings about Arianne through a hundred song titles: *You Go To My Head, I Got It Bad And That Ain't Good, Falling In Love With Love, That Old Black Magic,* and on and on. . . . But in the end it would probably be *You Always Hurt The One You Love.* So Sutton held back, gave Arianne a straight answer, leaving his lament for another time, smiling his crooked smile as he spoke softly about the country he loved.

He told her about the sun coming up golden over the Grand Canyon, the smell of the Atlantic Ocean, the thump of fireworks on Fourth of July, the sweep of mountains through the Rockies. He told her about the Arizona desert, a stark beauty, like a soul without flesh. And there was the sound of the wind through the pines of Georgia; the first snowfall of winter in New York City, tug boats chugging up the gray East River; and the moon over San Francisco Bay with the water shining like wavering tinsel on a sheet of black glass.

He told her about all the other sights and sounds that could have inspired a million other songs. As Sutton listened to himself he held Arianne's hand and kept his eyes closed, wondering at his own words—ramblings, impressions he never brought out before. He was amazed at himself and the affection he had for the things he spoke about. God, it seemed like a million years since he had been home. And suddenly his voice went hollow, sour notes from a busted horn. It was all so hopeless sometimes. America was so distant that it seemed foreign to him.

After a while they went up to the bedroom and undressed in silence. Sutton listened to her in the dark, the small simple sounds of her breathing, then the rustle of expensive silk undergarments against her smooth skin, the padding of her feet through the mottled shadows, her thighs slipping along cool sheets, her sigh when he took her in his arms.

Sutton held Arianne with an unrelenting tension that trembled through their bodies, and he did not say anything. But there in the dark, with Arianne as close as she could be, he was flooded with a deep longing for the things he loved—things that made him who he was.

FIVE

The next morning the sun came up vivid orange, less spectacular than yesterday's sunrise but a lot more hopeful for *The Beast*'s crew. They flew the practice mission down to Land's End then came around to starboard on the second leg, cruising along at 3,000 feet, viewing the patchwork with detached curiosity. Rowe bitched the whole time because they weren't getting credit for a mission: "But what the hell do I care, it ain't *my fucking* gasoline." None in the crew supported him, knowing that the claim was ridiculous even to imagine.

"Knock it off," Sutton told Rowe, tired of the crackle of Rowe's voice in his headphones. That sort of moaning was for other crews, not his, and he didn't want to hear anymore. If it was a legitimate claim he could have let them all pipe in and get it off their chests, but he wasn't going to stand for that sort of nonsense, not today. Sutton gazed out over the Bay of St. Ives, out over the Atlantic, instinctively checking for FWs and Bf-109s. He thought he saw one, but it was a mirage. It was eight-thirty, in New Jersey it would be one-thirty in the morning. Allison, snug in daisy-patterned sheets would be asleep, seven hours away from her job at dad's factory, certainly not preparing to type out a quick note to dear Jim. Sutton wondered too if Allison would even take a peek at the silver-framed photo of himself she claimed stood on her desk, a gift she begged for only last Christmas. Probably dating some handsome 4-Fer with a solid job and a big car for tooling down to the beach on weekends. They flew over the tin mines of Cornwall, with their white hills and pools of green-colored water, and then they were over freshly tilled soil and saw cyclists dotting the wandering roads, and flocks of pigeons flying nervously, much the way they did on a raid, and everywhere trees and crooked roads, not one more straight than an inch, so peaceful, so calm. Sutton saw *The Beast*'s shadow along pastures and beaches, a dim smudge of war skimming across British history. They roared over a castle and Sutton thought of his high school England: Sir Galahad, the sword plunged into stone, King Arthur, a knight's silver armor. And for a moment he longed for his childhood, the serenity that comes with innocence. There was comfort in these thoughts, but it was only momentary. Gibson's Midwestern drawl sliced through the interphone and announced the approach of the village that had been designated as the "target"—the area chosen for the practice mission.

They used a method of photography called Tri-metrogen. A camera mount under the floor of the bomber's radio compartment held three standard six-inch metrogen lens K-17 cameras. The focal planes were in a 60° angular relationship—thus the name Trimetrogen. With each exposure a horizon-to-horizon picture was obtained with a running overlap in the direction of flight.

Parker had assigned a 23-year-old acne-faced cameraman with the unlikely name of Colter Harrow, an Army Air Force sergeant, to do the picture taking, someone Tutone found next to impossible to accept because of his sullen disposition and rat-shaped features. Harrow was an arrogant bastard, an arrogance that came from the Branch Parker school of charm—a cut from the same cloth. Compounding Tutone's dislike for Sergeant Harrow was Tutone's belief that Parker had also sent Harrow along as a palace spy—someone who would report on the performance of *The Beast*'s crew. "Be careful," Tutone told the Chief, "Harrow's got to be a pipeline to old Irontail." But the Chief shrugged it off, not getting any strong vibrations confirming Tutone's feeling. Capping it off was Harrow's comment before climbing aboard prior to the practice mission.

Harrow had glanced at the ship's unusual splotchy camouflage paint scheme--a scheme that had prompted naming the bomber *The Beast*—and told Tutone that he thought the ship looked "like a real flying shithouse." The comment was an outrage, an insult. This was Tutone's ship and Harrow had insulted both with sincerity, and Tutone had taken it much the way he would if the man insulted his woman or a prized automobile.

"Hey!" said Tutone, poking Harrow's skinny chest with a finger. "This isn't one of them shitcan camera planes you pop around in, this is a real warbird with combat miles stacked higher than all them damn rolls of silly film you've taken. Apologize!"

"It's the way I feel," Harrow replied.

"I said apologize."

Harrow remained silent.

It developed into a pushing match, Tutone using both hands, Harrow fending off the action with canisters of film. The rest of the crew, Sutton included, stopped and watched for a moment, feeling some of the insult Harrow had either deliberately or unwittingly vented.

Harrow said, "I was kidding, all right."

Sutton stepped between them. "Knock it off." Then he looked at Harrow. "You might reconsider, Sergeant, if you get my drift."

"Yeah," Tutone said, looking over Sutton's shoulder.

"Parker said you guys were all nuts," said Harrow, not looking any of them in the eye.

Tutone spun around and said to the Chief, "See, I told you!"

The Chief nodded agreement.

Sutton said, "Well?"

Harrow embraced the canisters, tucking them close to his chest like armor plating, an ineffectual move. His small rodent eyes moved around nervously in his head like those of a frustrated squirrel. "Okay, I didn't mean it. I'm sorry."

"Then what the hell did you say it for?" asked Tutone.

"It was a game," Harrow said. "I mean, if you don't play games what fun is life?"

Less than an hour later they were up in the English air chasing their shadow while Harrow plucked away at apertures and film speeds. Griffin was aloof to the situation—to Harrow, what he said, Tutone's hurt feelings, Sutton and how he handled the matter. Griffin let the boys play while the men honored themselves with the real work of war. Griffin prepared himself not so much for the content of the mission, but the style— how he would look in Parker's eyes. He had set himself aside from "those people," as he referred to them in letters home. Then, just before they came over the practice target Sutton told Griffin to go back and check Harrow. So Griffin unbuckled himself and lumbered his way to the radio compartment under the flooring where Harrow sat perched over the K-17s like a mouse hugging his cheese.

Griffin nudged him. "Hey, everything all right?" he shouted. Harrow gave one of those responses you give someone without moving much of your body when you don't want to talk to them. Then Griffin shouted over the roar, "You have to get it right, Harrow!" And Harrow still did not respond, pretending to be overcome by his task. Griffin let up, thinking that Harrow was busy, not for a minute feeling that the fellow hunched over the cameras really didn't give a damn for him, that he didn't admire him. Roger was too consumed by himself to sense this because these moments seldom came to Griffin.

Roger Griffin achieved through money and guile and charm, not courage—which he was beginning to sense he lacked. So this was Griffin's discovery, a new vision of himself, a vision that filled him with a sense of emptiness. Some self-discoveries are painful, particularly this sort. It was not the war or the fear of combat or the possibility of death that surprised Griffin. It was Roger's realization of who and what he was that filled him with doubt and disappointment. Each of us has something special, a gift, a way, and we take this with us, using it or not; and when we discover that we have squandered our gift that is when we begin to fear who we are. Because in the end, we go alone, either filled with hope or angered with despair, and there comes a time, perhaps a moment, when we know who we really are. Griffin was approaching his with the same speed as the ship he was flying in.

The target run was near. Sutton must have announced it over the interphone because Harrow raised his hand, a signal for Griffin, then brought it back to the camera and said, "Go away. I don't need you." He started taking his pictures.

It was not until years later that Roger Griffin would sense the disassociation, the meaning of dislike, that he felt only partially at that moment. He cupped his blond head in his gloved hand and closed his eyes and waited for Sutton to call him back.

The Beast landed one hour later at Bassingbourn and rolled to a stop. Griffin had never felt so upset in his life, so alone, and he was the last to leave their ship. Tutone, with all his aplomb and verve, snapped away from the ship and headed toward a shower and a fresh uniform. He saluted Colonel Parker, approaching in a big olive-green four-door Chevrolet. Sutton fell through the forward hatch and was greeted by Parker, holding Rag Tag on a long leather leash. There was something similiar about the dog and old Irontail, Sutton thought. Rag Tag panted, glancing quickly between Sutton and Parker, checking out the remainder of the crew coming away from *The Beast;* his long tail thrashed impatiently on the warm tarmac. Rag Tag seemed to be waiting for Sutton's report.

Sutton rode with Parker to his office and talked about the mission and waited while the pictures developed. When Harrow came in he spread the photos on Parker's desk like pieces of the Holy Grail. The two stood looking at them saying positive things: "Nice." "Fine." "Sharp." "Fine contrast."

After Harrow left, Parker asked Sutton what he thought of the photographer.

Sutton said, "He's like a prophylactic—you hate to use it but it's the best thing around."

The photo mission to Pontoise was on for the day after tomorrow, so Parker gave Sutton's crew a twenty-four hour furlough; that was really swell of Parker because he was a cheap son of a bitch when it came to giving time off. Sutton said it was the last supper before the crucifixion, and no one disagreed with that statement.

Sutton, Griffin, Tutone, the Chief, Baker, and Kid Kiley, along with the officers from *Mona Wona* and *Firepower Inc.,* flew in a shiny new DC-3 up to Lancastershire that afternoon where they, along with a hundred other fliers, settled into what had once been a luxury hotel in the seaside resort of Southport, overlooking the Irish Sea. By seven o'clock they had a good American meal, fresh cigarettes, and lots of beer. They sat on the veranda and watched the sun change

71

the sea into a sheet of hammered gold; they did this mostly in silence, thinking about home and what they left—wondering about the future and what they faced. The place had a band and a solid vocal group which sang songs, sentimental beauties that reminded everyone of home and family and wives and girlfriends. The memories gave some of them the willies—particularly Kid Kiley, who had received a brutal "Dear John" letter from one Cissy McCabe. Kiley brandished the note—after four beers—like a white flag of defeat, reciting the missive with beery breath, punctuating the end with one final word—"Bitch!"

"Unlucky at love, lucky at war," Bo Baker said, and it seemed to have interested Kiley because his frown turned to an inquisitive smile.

"You mean to tell me," Kiley said, eyelids heavy with beer, "that if a guy gets one of these things he can survive this stinking war?"

"Natch," Baker said. "You can't lose at everything."

"I think I like that, yeah, I think I really do." Then Kiley took out a Zippo, spun the flintwheel and struck the flame under the letter while the others cheered him on. "Goodbye, dear Cissy." Everyone laughed except Griffin.

He said, "That's a crock of shit."

"How come you always know just the right thing to say," Baker said.

The group went silent and watched the flames consume the letter.

Griffin stood and looked down at them. "You guys live in a fantasy world. None of you ever makes any sense. Kiley here thinks he'll survive the war because some dame rejected him. The Chief over there believes

The Beast is some sort of sacred animal, blessed by some benevolent spirit that will take us through the end of this war untouched. And Rowe wears a flak jacket around his balls because he thinks they're the most precious things in the world. Tutone believes he's indestructible and loves the taste of combat like most men love women. It's as if nine loonies had been stuffed into one plane. And everytime we go up on a mission I've got to listen to your jive talk, always talking about how the other guy is going to get killed. Well, I've got news for you, Jack, you're all living in a fantasy world. It's *Alice In Wonderland,* that's what I think."

The beer had gotten to Griffin—or maybe it was the lunacy of combat or his own pent up fears, his dissappointment in himself and what he had discovered. He weaved, a punchdrunk fighter going down for the count. There had been sorrow in his voice and sorrow in his eyes, and the others saw it, wondered if maybe Roger Griffin, with all his money and all his fame, despite what his words had said, envied them. Because it was their craziness that bore them through this time in their young lives, that gave them the strength and impetus to fly. But to most of them, what Roger had said did not really matter; his was just another type of war wound. And for most of them sitting there, Roger's remarks would be remembered, yes, but most of all, he would be forgiven. That was their way.

Sutton loosened his tie and twisted the corner of his mouth the way he did, then leaned into the table. "And you, Griffin, what do you believe in?"

Griffin unbuttoned his jacket, picked up his cigarettes and said quietly, "Not a damn thing." Then he spun around and disappeared into the hotel.

Later, the band was playing *When You Wish Upon A Star.*

Sutton sat alone, listening.

"Hey," a sultry voice said behind him, "you look like hell."

Trisha Reed was a 23-year-old first lieutenant from Nevada, a WAAC ferry pilot who preferred to be called T.R.—"because it's got a spiffy ring to it." T.R. had flown practically everything in the Air Force inventory: *Thunderbolts,* P-38 *Lightnings,* the B-17, the B-24. She'd flown more types of aircraft—civilian and military—than any twenty men sitting on the veranda. She'd been flying since she was twelve, when other girls were experimenting with lipstick and stockings and high-heels. Her tall, tight figure caused men to stare, and to dream at the same time. When she could she would avoid their stares, sometimes feeling guilty for being so attractive, which she never took advantage of.

T.R.'s silky auburn hair caught some of the soft light coming off the Chinese lanterns and she sat next to Sutton and said, "I flew up here in a broken down *Spit.* Made a perfect landing, too. You should have seen it, Jim, it was a beaut." Her tone was confident, as it always was—more so than most of the male pilots Sutton knew.

Sutton smiled. "T.R., you know as well as I that any landing is a perfect landing."

"What happened to the gang?"

"Your pal the boy wonder scared them off."

"Hey, look, hotshot, just because I went out with the

74

guy doesn't mean I'm going to have his babies."

"Christ, I thought you were upside down in a cloud over ol' Rog."

"You must think that when it comes to men I'm a real egg."

"Egg, hell, I thought you were in love. Seems to me that every woman that meets Griffin thinks he's a swell fella."

"Now look here, Jim Sutton, I think I know what you're doing—you want me to tell you that I don't care for Roger."

"You don't have to do that," Sutton said, smiling broadly. "Everyone heard what you did to him in Parker's room. When the pistol flare exploded in the hot stove the world heard about it, and although I wasn't there, I can just picture Roger running out stark naked with soot all over his body. You're a real rascal, T.R."

"He had it coming. Now, listen, I'm not going to tell you that Roger's a penguin or anything, he's just okay that's all, maybe a little stuck on himself, and we don't go together and you know that."

"Sure."

"Then what's your point?"

"I don't have a point. I guess I just like to tease you. When are you going back to the States?"

"A couple of days from now. I've got a lot of stuff to do before I leave."

Sutton called a waiter and ordered a beer for T.R. "Then why'd you come up here tonight?"

T.R. sat back in her chair and folded her hands, looked down at her ankles. She said, "I came up here to see you."

Sutton turned rather quickly and looked at T.R.'s buff-colored skin, the earnest lips, the hazel eyes staring at him intently—the same expression she might have waiting for an overdue lover in a storm, that look of concern that seemed to come over people when they feel their vulnerabilities starting to show. In a moment T.R.'s facial expression changed, a subtle twist of muscle and emotion, a slight cocking of her head, the chin jutting forward. A gentle breeze threw a lock of hair across her brow. Now she had one of those looks straight from a fashion magazine where the model assumes that beckoning sensual look that you can only experience on a veranda near the Irish Sea when you let your imagination run crazy after a half-dozen beers and are looking for someone to care for you very much. Sutton could have disregarded the look but he was just as vulnerable as any of the other fliers, just as fearful, just as lonely.

He asked T.R., "What did you come up here for?"

"Jim, you know that I'm falling in love with you."

The answer was typical T.R., one of those rare, succinct, refreshing, clear sentences that, from most people, is too often an accident of tongue and brain. But the sentence summed her up. Another woman might have danced around the thought all evening, laying down a trail of lavender smoke and polished fingernails, imparting a feeling of unintended disillusion. But T.R. was honest, and that was something Sutton knew and that was what bothered him. T.R.'s words were clear, and with their ring came a responsibility that Sutton was not prepared to face. T.R. had spoken softly, a whisper, hushed by that sweaty vocal group over there painting a backdrop for scared hearts intuitively seeking the safety of romance, singing a dreamy arrangement of Cole Porter's *What Is This Thing Called Love?*

So for a few seconds, through the lilt of the verse, Sutton and T.R. stared at each other, filled with the wonder that comes at that inexplicable moment when the soul senses something consequential in the air. The moment of The Thunderbolt: two people sitting bathed in the mist of the Irish Sea while Chinese lanterns swayed to Cole Porter's precious poem of wonder and pertubation. What next, the heart might ask, who should speak? What could be said?

T.R. had subtly and distinctly placed her heart there on the table amid the ashes and beer bottles, an act she had only committed once before. But it had to come out; it was a feeling that had to be aired, a thought that needed venting in an otherwise reserved soul—this despite her confidence, her self-assured manner. Pure woman T.R. was, and still virginal, not because she had not yearned to lose that vestige of childhood, but because she had really never met anyone worthy of that special first-time sharing that only comes once. *The grand moment,* T.R. called it when speaking with a friend.

But moments come and moments go. This one now hovered; it did not ascend nor descend; it remained a balloon of emotion yearning to bust.

Another song now, this one Harold Arlen and Johnny Mercer's mystical, *That Old Black Magic,* circa 1942—timeless, alluring, passion-filled.

Somehow then they were holding hands, somewhere between the ashes, their hearts, the beer bottles. And while they did this, T.R. mouthed the lyrics as the vocal group sang. They danced on a floor the size of a calendar, very close, T.R.'s cheek pressed against Sutton's. She was the symbol of classic American good looks, the shape of the eternal woman, elemental, glorious, exciting. T.R.'s *citron* scented soap filled the air, and Sutton felt the warm breath from her lips ever so close to his ear as she softly continued with the murmuring words.

Allison was not like this; she had never made Sutton feel the way he did now—she was a real pill-head, never writing, dedicated to herself, and Arianne was . . . confusing.

Sutton admired T.R., respected her—and aside from undressing her in his mind once, there had been a distance, or a lack of time or opportunity for him to think anything desirous: it was T.R.'s self-confidence, self-respect and intelligence that intrigued him. But now, something else, something more basic was evolving. . . .

They stopped dancing.

Sutton grasped T.R.'s hand and looked beyond the glow of her eyes and wrapped his arms around her firm body. He said nothing. He closed his eyes and kissed T.R.'s waiting lips.

SIX

At Bassingbourn the next morning—0844—fresh-cut grass scented the air and the sky was a flier's dream: limitless and clear. The Englishman riding the tractor pulling the mower had passed *The Beast* when three Army Air Force jeeps halted long enough for the crew to spill out. A moment later, with Rag Tag trotting close behind, Colonel Parker arrived to start the mission off, appearing more sullen than usual. Sutton and Griffin dropped their gear under the nose section and looked up at Sergeant Holden, *The Beast*'s maintenance chief, standing near the Number 4 engine, his face and hands greasy smears.

"You guys can't fly this bird today," Holden said calmly, without the slightest tone of regret or respect for rank.

Holden had little regard for officers. For fifteen years he had fixed, screwed, tweaked, babied, kicked, and pacified every type of aircraft in the Army Air

Force; he knew their idiosyncracies by heart, the way some men know the feel of their women. If the Griffins and Suttons of the Air Force flew airplanes and won medals—or died trying—it was because the Holdens of the service made the planes fly. *The Beast* was Holden's—he was endeared to her mechanisms, her steel and gears and pumps and desires. When Sutton strapped *The Beast* on his back and took her up into the heavens, or one of the gunners swiveled a turret, they were borrowing Holden's pride, his effort. Not that the crew resented this, but at times Holden went too far. Like the time Bush accidently spit on one of the tires and later found the contents from a jar of honey in his flying boots.

Holden would have preferred *The Beast* to remain forever on static display, serving the public perhaps in a museum where the weather was controlled and understanding. If *The Beast* remained on the ground, Holden often said, nothing would break; if nothing broke, Holden would not have to sweat, poke or curse fixing her. And it didn't matter who or what broke *his* ship. German flak or German fighter pilots firing metal objects into his bird were just as susceptible to his outrage and virulent tone as some damned green American flier who happened to prang his ship on the runway.

Sutton cocked his head back and shaded his eyes from the sun's glare and said to Holden, "What's the problem?"

Holden squatted on the wing, an oil rag in one hand, the other poking an open panel. "Oil leak. A big one."

"Oil leak!" Sutton shouted back. "What the hell

kind of oil leak? You were supposed to check that yesterday."

Shrugging his shoulders, Holden said: "Yesterday, Captain, there was no oil leak. Today there's an oil leak. If you want, you can climb into your little cockpit and push the buttons and fly this thing right off the ground. But if you do that, you and the dear Lord are going to have a meeting at the end of the runway."

Tutone swaggered over looking like a school boy who had his little red wagon taken away for the day. "Where's the leak?" he demanded.

"The leak," Holden told them, caressing the side of the engine, "is somewhere in here."

"Brilliant," Tutone said, "absolutely brilliant." He turned to Sutton and added, "He's got to be working for the Germans, boss."

"Can you be more specific, Sergeant?" Parker asked.

Holden stood again and wiped his hands on his thighs. "Sir," he said, looking at Parker and ignoring the others, "I can't locate the source of the leak so I'm going to take the engine off. It'll take quite a few hours to do the job. In the meantime, these boys would look awful silly flying a four-engine plane with only three engines."

Parker took a few moments and realized there was a chance he'd have to scrap the mission. Griffin walked over and tried to take charge of the conversation, trying to show everyone he was an oil leak specialist, that he'd seen plenty of this type problem. But soon it was apparent that Holden, ever faithful and always accurate, was indeed telling the truth. Parker had to have a second opinion so he summoned Sergeant

81

Beckworth, the chief wrench from Captain Chrisp's ship, supposedly the most meticulous and knowledgeable mechanic on the base.

Beckworth, built like a mechanical pencil, wore spotless coveralls and walked like a man from Rolls-Royce or Jaguar—the nose and head tilted back slightly, the shoulders stiff and square. There wasn't a spot of grease to be seen on his scrubbed pinkish skin and his boots shone jewel-like; his accent was New England with a dash of British around the edges, and his mannerisms were as sharp as the creases on his coveralls. Beckworth conferred with Holden for a couple of minutes, walked up the ladder to the top of the wing, smeared some of the suspicious oil on his immaculate fingers, sniffed it like a bloodhound, then shook his head slowly. He looked up at Holden and they spoke for a while, a few long paragraphs of engine talk, two doctors discussing brain surgery.

Parker stood by impatiently. Anxiety marked his face—like the father of the surgical patient expecting bad news at any second. While Beckworth and Holden conferred, Parker ordered Litton to check the availability of another bomber for today's mission.

After nearly five minutes of probing, touching, gazing, and tapping, Beckworth and Holden stood after finally agreeing on a diagnosis.

Beckworth said, "It's an oil leak, Colonel."

"No shit," sung Tutone, throwing his hands into the air.

The prognosis, Beckworth told the trio after he stepped down from the ladder, was that the patient would recover in due time, that a seal had somehow popped or that a hairline fracture had occurred

82

through fatigue. To be safe the engine would have to be lifted and taken apart to determine the true cause.

A ripple of elation swept over the crew, particularly Rowe who would use a hangnail as an excuse to remain on the ground.

An hour later they passed over the French coastline in a nameless silver B-17G that was so new it still smelled of the factory. The ship sparkled like an unwrapped toy, a bomber without combat time, just recently checked out and tested through the security of English air. Each of the crew—from Griffin back to Kid Kiley—knew that when they stepped into one of these bombers their lives rested with their pilot and their own ability as a crew. Over the period of weeks that they'd flown together the crew had come to trust Sutton and each other. But out here in the war zone new *Fortresses* bared aspects of their souls that no test crew under non-hostile conditions could ever detect. And that's what gave Sutton and the others a bad case of the willies—they were waiting for something to go wrong, for a fuel pump to fail, a control surface to jam—especially the Chief with his uncanny sense for these things. Unlike *The Beast,* this ship didn't have the Chief Whitefeather Seal of Official Indian Approval. Any evil spirits in *The Beast* had been dispelled by this shapeless amulet. *The Beast* had been approved by all and she was a good ship so that when they took her into the air, regardless of the conditions, they placed their faith in her like men placing their faith in a good honest woman.

Sergeant Litton had done his job, had found this ship they were flying in, passed its number along to

83

Parker right there in front of *The Beast* moments before Beckworth and Holden had stated she was unfit for flight.

Litton: shaped like a pear, he was one of those people who relished life's gruesome, unpleasant tasks. When fliers were killed Litton would pick through their personal effects before shipping them to the next of kin, hoping each time to find something incriminating —a letter from a lover, a prophylactic, a pornographic picture—that, instead of discarding, he could keep for himself. It was also Litton who had the sour task of waking fliers in Sutton's barracks each morning before a mission; that steely voice sang out with pleasure, rousing the troops, aware that it wasn't he that would take to the air, but *them*. Litton was Parker's pipeline, the conveyor of bad news, the town crier who always had something negative to announce. He was a manipulator, a sergeant who skillfully hid behind the power of Parker's rank and knew how to use it to his advantage. So it wasn't unusual that Litton had discovered the one available ship for Sutton's crew. He passed its number to Parker through a whisper so that the crew, instead of remaining grounded with their sick ship, would once again have a chance at dying.

The last thing Sutton saw before he wheeled this new ship onto the taxiway was Litton—smiling, standing beside Parker and his jerky dog. Sutton kept the image in his head like a photograph.

Up here in the air now at 13,000 feet at an indicated airspeed of 150 MPH in this nameless bird with ten nervous crewmen fifteen minutes from their target, Benny Tutone depressed his interphone button and swiveled his turret slowly around and around.

"You can't win, boss," Tutone said to Sutton, knowing the rest of the crew listened. "Reminds me of a story of this ant I watched one day."

"A *what?*" asked Sutton.

"An *ant*. Did you know that an ant can lift a hundred times its own weight? Anyway, the ant crawls out from some grass into a dirt clearing about the size of a plate and spots a dead cricket. First, the ant checks the area out with his feelers, testing the air, the vibrations, for any hostile shit that might be around. When he felt everything was all right he rushed toward the cricket and grabbed a leg and started tugging. I mean, he really starts jerking the thing, trying to pull it backwards. But the damned cricket is wedged between two pebbles."

"Two *what?*"

"Two pebbles—boulders to the ant. But the ant doesn't give up, see, he let's go of the cricket and starts pushing the pebbles away. First the one on the left, then the one on the right. It takes a while and you can sense that the ant is sweating his little ant's ass off. Anyway, after he gets everything clear he goes back to the cricket and starts pulling backwards again. Every once in a while he stops for a breather, runs around clears more pebbles. You can tell that nothing is going to get in the ant's way, that he's going to get the damned cricket back to his ant hole so everybody can have lunch. Finally he has a nice clear shot and pulls the cricket right up to his ant hole and stops dead. Just then a bird flies down and picks up the cricket in its beak and disappears. You should have seen the look on the ant's face."

While the crew laughed Kid Kiley asked, "Did you really see that happen?"

"Would Benny Tutone, the world's greatest living gunner, bullshit you?"

Kiley said, "When did you see it happen?"

"Last night. Just before I woke up."

Through their laughter Gibson announced that they had twelve minutes before the target. The interphone went silent again and then someone said: "I never liked birds."

At that moment at Orly Airfield a shiny emerald green BMW convertible slipped to a halt a few yards away from two parked FW-190s. The car had a windscreen, chrome trimmed and separated by a vertical chrome strip. The black vented hood was secured by two large brown leather straps pulled taut from one side to the other. The vented wheels—also emerald green and highly polished—were capped in chrome but did not bear the distinctive black and white BMW logo which shone atop the long split grill. The chromed bumpers and headlight rims of the car were spotless and sparked brilliantly in the glare of the morning sun.

The car's driver, a handsome athletic man with swept-back sandy colored hair and deep blue eyes, stepped slowly from the BMW and closed the door gently. This was his private automobile and he cherished it, a gift to himself a year ago on his twenty-eighth birthday. This morning the driver was not wearing his tan summer flying suit; he chose to wear his blue-gray four-pocket Service Tunic with matte aluminum buttons, standard Luftwaffe collar and shoulder rank insignia denoting the rank of *major,* and the Luftwaffe's version of the national emblem over the right breast pocket. The Knight's Cross with Oak Leaves hung around his neck over the knot of his tie. Above his left breast pocket, the Operational Flying Clasp of a fighter pilot. The Pilot's Badge was pinned in the center of his pocket: an eagle with outstretched wings and swastika clasped in its claws was a black finished metal. The driver wore bulky flying boots and pants; his service cap (without the rigid cap spring it appeared crushed) was cocked back and down the side of his head at a rakish angle, and now he crossed his arms and inspected the sky with the eyes of a pensive eagle. His name was Georg-Peter Eder and there was an elegance to the way he stood.

Eder's passenger in the right front seat had also moved silently away from the convertible and stood and stared silently at the waiting Focke-Wulfs. Although the men had come here together they now, for the moment, stood apart. The passenger was similiarly dressed but he was thinner than Eder and much shorter and very young: 26 years old, the most highly decorated and youngest *major* in the Luftwaffe. If Eder was the shape of elegance, this young *major* seemed arrogant, almost defiant. But most of this had been tempered: arrogance was changing to confidence, defiance to pride. August Baerenfaenger was his name and he was a national hero.

A month ago in a captured English *Spitfire,* Baerenfaenger had flown from a base in France and singlehandedly strafed Bassingbourn, destroying several B-17s. More than anything, the action was a morale booster for both the Luftwaffe and the German people. It earned Baerenfaenger the Diamonds to his Knight's Cross, bestowed on him by Hitler in a much-publicized ceremony in Berlin. But because of his "star status," Baerenfaenger was taken off flying status to preserve his life and to promote the Luftwaffe while recruiting young fliers. He flew guard escort for Hugo Sperrle the same day he was awarded the Diamonds, the same day Sutton and his crew had attempted to shoot down Sperrle.

Eder and Baerenfaenger walked to the near fighter, the ship with the number '13' scribed in black on the dappled flanks, the great sleek knight's horse that would fling its rider through the heavens, shattering nature with an awful mechanical scream. Here they stopped. A *hauptfeldwebel* dressed in black fatigue coveralls came up behind them with a Leica camera and they posed.

With their silver braid and silver metal-and-canvas parachute harnesses, lean, hard, against the shape of steel in which they fought, they projected a dangerous aura—an aura not really human, but the apotheosis of their race caught for an instant by a thunderclap.

In less than twelve minutes the sky would have them, directed by a nameless voice speaking through their headsets, vectoring them toward a nameless silver bomber flown by a crew listening to a story about a bird and an ant.

SEVEN

"Check in," said Sutton from the pilot's seat of the unfamiliar *Fortress,* and he began to count each of them off, and as he did he yearned for his old trusted ship, *The Beast.* The thought gave him comfort because he loved her, not in Tutone's erratic way or the way the Chief thought of her as a good luck charm, but because *The Beast* was familiar and reliable, not uncertain and unknown like this ship. As Sutton steered he felt like a captain sailing a ship cut from fresh lumber.

"Okay," Rowe said.

David Rowe would be in the bombardier's seat, leaning forward in his tense way. In front of him, the conical Plexiglas windshield with its horseshoe-shaped glass panel, and before this the famous Norden bombsight, so classified, so sacrosanct, that it had to be removed personally by the bombardier after each flight and taken away like the hallowed son of a god king, cradled in Rowe's arms until safety had been secured. There were low windows in the compartment on both sides of Rowe. The post-and-ring sight for the Bendix chin turret hung above his head. Just now he would be ready, hunched over the wonderous Norden like a chunky Panda in his lamb's wool-lined flying suit, the floor, the lower walls, lined with those ever-present flak jackets systematically placed to protect, not the Norden, but Rowe's groin. This compartment was the point of the blade, the gunsight for every mission, the reason for being. To Rowe's left on the wall was the bomb rack control salvo release, the bombardier's window wiper motor, and to the rear of these the bomb door retracting lever and the bombardier's panel equipment. Near this, the bombardier's panel light, a goose-necked lamp that might have served a peaceful function in a child's room. The Norden was ready and Rowe took a quick peek through the eyepiece then glanced over at the picture of Hedy Lamarr—a publicity shot from the motion picture, *White Cargo,* 1942. Hedy, wonderful Hedy, propped up on one elbow, one hand grasping a beaded necklace, a luscious leg stretched out, the eyes seductive and sensual, the mouth half open.

Behind Rowe was Gibson's compartment, which he referred to as his office. He had his own desk—the manual called it the navigator's table—and this was against the left wall so that when he sat there he flew sideways unless he swiveled his chair around to face forward. In front of him was the RS-2 rack selector relay. Rowe was embedded in a cocoon of metal and instruments, and at the rear end of his table, which ended at bulkhead Number 3, there was an array of dials, boxes, tubing, and wire harnesses. It was not a place for people with claustrophobia, but neither was it as cramped as the upper and belly turrets. There was the interphone jack box, the radio compass junction box, a hook for the headset, and a cartridge box chute. Against the bulkhead near the ceiling was the radio compass control box, ammunition boxes, the heating and ventilating ducts, and the signal light box. The most prized piece here was a black and white snapshot, taped to the wall in front of Gibson's head: a pretty 18-year-old girl cuddling a white Irish Terrier named Honey—a gift from Gibson. On the table near Gibson's charts were two Hershey bars and an unopened pack of Wrigley's gum. Everything was neatly arranged, and Gibson would dust the area whenever he felt his compartment in *The Beast* was getting messy.

The section beyond the bulkhead, a half level above, housed the pilot's compartment, accessible through a trapdoor from Gibson's compartment between the pilot and copilot's seat. Spread out in front of Sutton and Griffin—Sutton on the left, Griffin on the right— was a vast display of instruments. Between them, the control panel and pedestal: ignition switches, fuel boost pump, landing gear and wing flap switches, turbo-supercharger controls, throttle and mixture controls. Altogether there were over a hundred and fifty dials, gauges, levers, switches, buttons, knobs, and cranks—and at any second one of them could either save or lose the entire crew.

In back of the cockpit, behind Griffin and Sutton, was the engineer's area. Benny Tutone was in the upper turret now, revolving the dome-shaped, glassed, half ball slowly around. This he did to observe as well as keep the oil warm. When he wasn't acting as the aircraft's flight engineer, Tutone was in the turret, where he felt more at home. Within it there was barely room for Tutone's head and shoulders. From the metal-ribbed Plexiglas protruded the twin .50-caliber barrels. Under power the turret moved on a cogged track, while the guns were fired through an automatic computing sight. Elevation and depression was activated through an electrical mechanism. Since Tutone had been a drummer, it was easy for him to coordinate the movements of the turret—he needed both hands and both feet to work it effectively. Two handles charged the guns with ammunition and the two hand grips controlled the azimuth and elevation; the triggers were located on them also, and a range knob was set between them. There were other gadgets for heat, oxygen and communications, as well as a hand crank in the event of a power failure. And of course, all these devices had to be manipulated with lightning speed while under attack, and the chance for death was very real if the operator missed a beat. Dangling from a thick strand of spaghetti wiring was Tutone's St. Christopher's medal. It was a crude but effective indicator that, from the corner of his eye, he came to trust in more ways than he cared to admit.

Corporal Bo Baker owned the radio room aft of the pilot's compartment. He was a neat housekeeper, and although he missed *The Beast,* he admired this room because it was spotless and freshly painted—it reminded him of the smell of a new car. This was a self-contained room, the only such place in a B-17. Baker could shut the doors to both the forward and aft bulkheads and pretend he was in a small cabin cruising above mainland America. To get here from the engineer's compartment one had to walk across the catwalk through the bomb bay. In here were the bomb hoist bracket, the bomb rack and shackle, the bomb rail, and a wide assortment of valves, pumps, and fuel transfer lines. Baker's office was next, with its own table and multitude of VHF, liaison sets, interphone, marker beacon, radio altimeter, radio compass recorder, and homing set. Everything was stacked around the room. Baker loved to read and write, and once Sutton saw him writing a letter, firing his gun, writing, oblivious to the threat of death. And that would be Sutton's everlasting impression of Baker: a man composing a letter and occasionally trying to bag a German fighter.

Next came the ball turret, like an inverted cup set in its socket in the bottom of the ship. Between this and the upper turret, there was one major difference. Skolinsky, the ball gunner, had to slip in, much like a rodeo cowboy sitting down on a horse in a chute before the gate opened. Once down, he assumed the fetal position, an embryo pose, firing his guns between his legs, the door locked above him, the turret not only revolving in azimuth, as did the upper turret, but also in elevation, which the upper turret couldn't do. Skolinsky literally moved up and down and around with the exact motion of the turret. It was a vulnerable, scary place, a position for possible entombment. Unlike the upper turret, his mechanisms were more complex than Benny Tutone's. To adjust the recticles of his gunsight for range, Skolinsky used his left foot pedal; to talk on his interphone, he used his right foot; he tracked the target with hand grips and fired the guns with switches atop them; and the turret door could only be unlocked when the ball was properly upright. Before every mission Skolinsky would go to each crewmember and make them swear to unlock him if he ever got stuck. He would have nightmares of being trapped, a bird inside a jar while a hunter took aim with a powerful gun. It was the most miserable position in the ship.

The waist gunners' posts came after Skolinsky. They were located in the longest section of the aircraft, honeycombed walls with frames and ribbing: the Chief on the right, Bush on the left. The windows they fired from were open, without glass or doors, and they were staggered so that the gunners were almost side-by-side and not interfering with each other's motion. The Chief, because of his seniority over Bush, had tacitly claimed this area as his. Bush, a rather aggressive sort, wasn't easily agitated by people but he had acquiesced to the Chief's experience and knowledge—the student showing admiration for the professor. With three German fighters to his credit, the Chief was readily admired by young gunners fresh from the States.

In the final bulkhead behind a doorway in the tail of the bomber Kid Kiley stubbed out a Lucky Strike. There were two ways to enter Kiley's compartment: from the tail wheel compartment through a small door in the bulkhead; the other way was through a door in the fuselage not far from the Chief's side of the bomber. The equipment here was sparse—ammunition boxes, a seat, the interphone jack, and the suit heater outlet provided with a rheostat control; also, there were two oxygen regulators on each wall. When Kiley actually fired his guns he perched on his seat, pressed his body rearward and kneeled on a pair of knee pads. His twin fifties were fired using a ring-and-post sight hanging on pulleys and cables. After a mission Kiley's compartment would be littered with cigarette butts and candy and gum wrappers. Once he had taken an entire fried chicken with him and neatly stacked the bones on the floor.

Sutton now completed his check and told everyone to knock off the chatter and called down to Colter Harrow. Until then, Harrow had been sharing Baker's private cabin, flying along in the auxilliary crew member's seat; a couple of minutes ago he had moved down into his cameraman's position situated under the floor of the radio compartment. He had a small seat, and in front of this was the camera door latch.

"Harrow," Sutton said, "do you have the door open?"

"Yes, sir."

Gibson said, "We've got about sixty seconds before the target."

"All right, keep your eyes peeled," said Sutton. "Harrow, wait for Gibson's signal then start running the camera. Everyone else keep on the lookout for fighters."

"Fighters!" Tutone said, affecting a lisp: "No one told me this would be dangerous. Stewardess! Oh, stewardess!"

EIGHT

Gibson checked his chronometer.

"Five seconds."

Now they began searching, each crew member checking the sky for fighters and checking the ground for whatever they were supposed to uncover. Every man had a sector he was responsible for in the event of attack. The book told them that each man would cover his own area and that—at least hypothetically—if this were done properly they would be safe from attack, but they had flown together long enough to realize that it helped to check the other guy's area also, an action for mutual safety, and an unwritten law of the Brotherhood. This opened a can of worms because everyone under attack began talking at once, so at times it was impossible to make any sense of the language. It was a difficult situation to control.

"Roll the camera," Gibson told Harrow.

When the crew heard this they took their eyes out of

the sky and began to check the ground. Pontoise was distinct: a wedge-shaped village with the taller buildings arced around the wider portion of the wedge, the small structures tapering down to the narrow point. Around the town, typical French fields, pastures, and winding roads that snaked off into the horizon.

"Maybe that's what we're after," Rowe said into the interphone, referring to small clumps dotting the pastures—straw colored heaps, like stacks of hay before they were baled.

"Could be," Sutton said, "but you shouldn't be looking down there. Check for fighters."

As Sutton searched he thought of Arianne and T.R., of Allison and her little pink slippers patting along the kitchen floor, and he thought of the surprise he felt when T.R. appeared at Southport, perky and bouncy, announcing that she cared for him. *Who do you care for the most?* he wondered. *The girl in New Jersey who never writes, who'll be there if I get home, because she's that way. She wants to be with a flier, to tell her friends that Jim's returned from the big bad war, feeling some glory through association. And then, a couple of weeks after, she'll probably* . . .

The hell with it—

"Harrow," Sutton said, "are you getting all this? I sure as shit hope you are. Do you want another run? I don't want to have to come back here if the pictures are lousy. Harrow? Are you listening to me?"

"We've got some good pictures, Captain, you can head home now," Harrow announced.

Tutone said, "Yeah, good idea, let's take a heading for LaGuardia Airfield, fuck this war. Gibson—hey, man, taking a heading for New York and have the stewardess bring old Benny a big tall one, and a fat pillow for his weary head."

Griffin swiveled around in his seat straining against his shoulder harness and glared at Tutone. "Shut up, damn it!" The words were propelled by frustration, not anger. Griffin had begun to show more of himself, going about it in his own odd way, trying to cover his fear like all the other fliers did.

Sutton always tried to remain icy cool.

Tutone had his bravado, his sense of humor.

The Chief had his mystical spirits, personal gun-bearers that fired at anything he deemed repulsive.

Rowe had sex and a mistrust of everything.

Baker had his books and letters and his reclusive nature.

"I want you all to shut up," Sutton curtly told them.

Then he banked left and the wing went down and the big silver ship without a name wheeled over the outer boundary of Pontoise, beautifully photographed from the air, until Sutton leveled her at 5,000 feet, taking a heading for Bassingbourn from Gibson. He felt glad that no one cared enough to try to shoot them down.

Fifteen minutes later Kid Kiley came on the interphone. "Got two fighters coming in."

"That's just fucking ducky," Griffin said, the sound of the word *fighters* cutting through his ears, and for an instant everything stopped: the possibility of living, the damned war, his heart. Everything but that ugly word singing in his brain. *Fighters!*

They came over the top too far off to fire at, their wings twisting and spiraling, their sleek frames streaking against pure blue—objects of cool perfection which Sutton admired because he knew how hard it was to fly those little bastards. Sutton neither hated them nor loved them—and he was sure they felt the same about him. But their motions were magical, a dance of the experts, the vision only lasting for seconds, a dot of time, and the impression deep and lasting. Two of them came up from the safety of the earth pushing themselves to meet the enemy. And who could say that they were much different than the ten American men riding in the nameless bomber?

Baerenfaenger and Eder were at full throttle and came over the top of the *Fortress* from behind. "Turn," Eder ordered, and Baerenfaenger's ship followed like a slick shadow, banking left and away from the bomber. Then it turned into the plane's direction, coming over the top, lining up for a frontal attack. "Good," Eder said, watching Baerenfaenger in his peripheral vision.

In an instant, with enough experience to his credit, Griffin watched the two fighters in the windscreen and knew they were good, not two green pilots busting through a cloud daring each other. Instead they were polished professionals who had practiced this exercise over and over in combat and were earnest and deadly. The maneuver was an awesome sight, neat and precise. "They're coming straight at us!"

There was a tone of alarm in Griffin's voice—almost a panic that none of the crew had heard before. The sentence was directed at Tutone, Rowe, and Skolinsky because they could train their guns directly at the charging fighters.

Baerenfaenger held a tight formation at Eder's eight o'clock position, sweeping down, a shallow dive, aiming toward the five o'clock sector of the American bomber that twinkled bright silver under the sun's strong rays.

"Tracers," Griffin announced, calmer now, realizing that there was nothing to do—a passive combatant relying on the expertise of three gunners, hoping the two German pilots might have a bad day.

The air filled with a series of long, streaking lights, an exchange of tracers. The bomber trembled with jackhammer jerks as the guns fired, trying to catch the planes.

Then something new happened—something no one had seen before.

As if they had flown into an apparition, a deadly nightmare.

Rowe spotted it first.

"Mother of God!" he said excitedly, "It blew up . . . no . . . wait . . . it didn't . . . a big flash on the fighter . . . the whole plane hidden for a second . . . Jesus!" Rowe gave his reports in a clear, flat-toned way for the benefit of the crew who could not see what he described. "Both of them seemed to ignite then reappear through their own flash . . . and then a shell seemed to fly at us. Did you guys see that . . . a couple of shells . . . one from each ship?" The fighters vanished and Rowe went on, reporting what he'd seen in a cool, objective fashion, hardly believing his own words. "I never saw anything like that before."

"All right, calm down," Sutton told him. "Keep your eyes peeled, they might be coming back."

Silence filled the ship, a sense of fear. This mysterious new weapon upset them. Enemy fighters with large-caliber cannons were familiar.

"The sons of bitches," murmured the Chief. The Germans were playing dirty, cheating at war.

Finally, Griffin spoke for all of them. "What the hell was that?"

"A rocket," Sutton announced. "An air-to-air rocket."

"A what?" asked Bush.

"A small rocket mounted on the wings."

Bush cut in. "I never heard of such a thing."

"Whatever the hell it was," Kid Kiley said, speaking calmly, "you're going to get a second peek because the bastards are coming back at eight o'clock and climbing."

"Keep sharp," Sutton said. "Keep with them."

The ships Eder and Baerenfaenger flew were FW-190A-7s and Sutton's assessment of the weapon was only partially correct.

The fighters circled out, preparing to double back for a flank attack against the bomber's starboard side.

What Baerenfaenger had fired was not technically called a rocket—it was a *mortar*. Eighty FW-190A-7s were produced prior to the end of 1943 and half of this number were designated R2 *Zerstorers:* within this grouping, some were further designated R6 models fitted with Wfr.Gr. 21 mortars. The launcher tube was 51.2 inches long and had three guide rails on the inner surface of the tube. When the bomb release button on the control column was depressed the mortar fired. After initial acclimation, rocket-equipped FW-190s worked successfully against the 8th Air Force daylight bomber formations. In one raid the fighters broke up a 228-aircraft B-17 formation, inflicting nearly 50 per cent losses. But by the time the R6 came into production the Luftwaffe had to contend with American fighters before attacking the B-17s. Also, when the rocket tube was attached the aerodynamic qualities of the nimble fighter deteriorated and their use was ultimately discontinued.

Now Eder and Baerenfaenger attacked from below and ahead of Sutton's ship.

"Give more lead time," Eder instructed Baerenfaenger, the American bomber in his sight. He estimated distance, the ship's speed. He steadied the fighter's wings and eased the gunsight on the bomber's belly section and fired.

Bush, Skolinsky, and Rowe were firing their guns but the fighters moved at a low, sweeping trajectory, forming a negative arch, the bomber's shells splattering the sky and falling earthward, narrowly missing the two planes zooming up.

"It's coming at me," Skolinsky said. "The rocket's coming right at me! Get me out of here, help me!" He sounded deranged, totally *non compos mentis.*

What Skolinsky had seen—what they all had seen—was a vision of mystery made stronger by repetition. The first blinding enigmatic flash a minute ago, the disappearance of the fighters, their emergence from an orange ball of hellish fire, had been accentuated this second time. It was a super weapon more capable of death now that each of them had seen its capability. It had been fired at Skolinsky and came at him with more vengeance, more hatred, more lethality than anything he'd ever seen.

It was deadly accurate.

Skolinsky did not stop screaming until the mortar hit.

The sound was earsplitting and it seemed to cut through the metal braces and spars like an enormous ax slicing through an oil drum. Two distinct sounds were almost simultaneous. But the loudest was Skolinsky's silence.

The Chief had been splattered with small bits of shrapnel and had a glove blown off. Bush, in a firing stance, was hit in the right arm and leg; he could feel a warm liquid against his skin.

Skolinsky began to gurgle, then his mike went dead.

Sutton ordered Griffin and Baker to go back and help.

While Rowe tended to the Chief and Bush, Griffin squatted over the belly turret. "Christ, there's a big hole on one side and . . . there's hardly anything left of the—"

"Do what you can. The rest of you stay with the fighters," said Sutton.

Skolinsky's head was tilted back and his eyes were open, shining like polished porcelain. The turret's glass was blown away with jagged fragments stuck in the torn and bent frames.

"His legs are gone!" Griffin couldn't believe what he was staring at. "Do you hear me? For God's sake, I said his legs are gone!"

Sutton tilted the *Fortress* over into a dive through a cloudless sky with the two fighters riding behind and Kid Kiley and Benny Tutone firing while Griffin hung on to the doorway on hands and knees near the massive wreckage, mesmerized by the torn remains of Skolinsky. Griffin tried to reach down into the turret but the angle of the dive was too severe.

"They're leaving," Kid Kiley said, watching the

fighters peel away, low on fuel.

Griffin inched over the turret's edge like a man leaning over a bloody manhole. Skolinsky's torso was twisted, most of his clothing had been blown or burnt off, and his eyes were open in a trance. His forearms rested on thighs, the hands palms-up as if waiting for salvation to release him from this, his ultimate misery. Griffin had never been so disgusted in his life. He reached down under Skolinsky's arms and tried to lift him from the wreckage, from the blast of the slipstream as they headed home. Skolinsky's legs had been severed at the knees without benefit of surgical precision—without sympathy or kindness, without reason. He had been trapped inside his steel and glass ball as in his nightmares.

"What happened back there?" Sutton asked Griffin.

"Skolinsky's dead."

Shock is temporary relief from reality and the sight of Skolinsky had anesthetized Griffin, given him welcomed countershock. He glanced up, his handsome blue eyes glazed like shiny stones. "He's dead." The sentence did not have a tone of finality but a tone of disbelief—as if it were a question with a less obvious answer.

Griffin had to move away; there was nothing else he could do. He helped Rowe working on Bush and the Chief, as efficiently as they could, applying first aid. Their wounds were not serious, and while they sat there there was an unspoken rule: no one looked into the turret.

The *Fortress* passed over the French coastline and a feeling of positive relief swept through the crew because they knew in a short while they'd be home. But halfway over the Channel, where the sea was brown and the waves snapped a frothy white, the heat of their mood cooled into a black gloom. In minutes they would have to face it: Skolinsky was dead.

By the time they landed their feelings had diffused. Baker, later that day in a letter to his mother, would refer to the incident as *a time of long and profound silence—as if each of us were both thankful and saddened; thankful that it was he, Skolinsky, who had been killed, and not one of us; saddened that one of our family had died.*

Each of them went through de-briefing—a special one that Parker had hastily organized with Major Marks and an officer from Wing Intelligence, Captain John Chimera.

NINE

"I want a desk job. A nice quiet pile of boring papers," Sutton told Chimera.

"You aren't serious, I'm sure," Chimera said, his observation accurate. After a couple of aborted attempts to become an engineer, Chimera had graduated from Columbia University's School of Architecture in New York City six months before Pearl Harbor. Tall and slim, prematurely bald, he appeared older than his twenty-six years. Parker had brought him down from Wing for a special reason.

"Maybe I'm not," Sutton said, "but sometimes it becomes unbearable up there."

"I'm sure," Chimera agreed, squinting through the smoke coming off a cigarette between taut determined lips.

"I saw the end of the war today, that's what I saw. The damned Germans have a secret weapon and today they used it."

Parker said, "That's not what Captain Chimera—"

"I know what the captain wants, Colonel," Sutton said. He reached out and took a sip of Scotch and said to Chimera, "There was a huge flash, a flame really, that seemed to envelope the wingman. We thought we had scored, that we hit a fuel tank or something, you know how it happens—an explosion, then pieces of airplane appear after the flash subsides. But this time, Jesus—this time the ship appeared intact after the flash and an object about twice the length of this desk came toward us."

"Obviously a rocket," Parker said.

"Obviously," Chimera replied, looking at Sutton. "Please continue."

Sutton slumped down in his chair, his brown eyes watery, gazing at the ceiling. "It missed, went wide and low, by how much I really can't say, maybe a hundred feet. I lost sight of it."

"Then what happened?" asked Parker.

"They came around again and got Skolinsky."

Chimera had the uncanny ability to analyze a situation by drawing on fact, logic, prior experience, and book knowledge. He could assimilate, compute, rationalize —both intuitively and professionally—and then succinctly place on the table a precise, well-packaged answer to a problem that seemingly had no solution. That was his way.

He had been stretched out in one of Parker's polished mahogany chairs and seemed totally relaxed, cool in thought, while the wheels buzzed like the inside of a finely oiled machine. During the process he smoked, the cigarette burning in Parker's brass ashtray. The ash, four minutes long now, was dangerously nearing the end, but Chimera took it away for one final satisfying deep draw that seemed to singe his fingers. He stubbed the stunted remains and lit another, the tenth in the past hour.

Parker had been put off by this erudite young man from New York City. Chimera wasn't typical Army Air Force, but somewhere under his shiny pate an answer was brewing that would effect the outcome of the May 24th raid on Paris, a mission that would pass over Pontoise—either successfully or disastrously. So there had to be limits to Parker's impatience as Chimera, blue eyes squinting in thought and the skin around the temples drawn in lines of concentration, pondered the matter.

Occasionally a seemingly inconsequential question came out. "Today's date is what?"

Parker checked his desk calendar. "May 20th."

Time passed like this, Parker toying with a Liberty Head silver dollar, those tense, tiny eyes of his flickering around the office nervously. Marks, very subdued, fidgeted on Parker's dark green sofa with the moth-ball scent, having already given them his opinion. Rag Tag also sensed the tension here because he was sitting up, wide-mouthed and panting, little flecks of saliva on his lips, staring vacantly at his master. At one point a bug crawled along the varnished floorboards toward the door and the dog cocked its massive head and tried, vainly, to paw it to death; but the bug was too swift, too intent on leaving this place.

Chimera again, with another question: "What time is the May 24th mission set for?"

"Twelve hundred hours, barring inclement weather. Listen, can I ask you a question?" said Parker.

Chimera smiled, one of his sly grins.

Parker took the silent cue. "All right, we've been here"—he checked his watch—"nearly an hour and five, no, six minutes. You've been through the interrogation, you've seen the photographs, you've heard my theory and listened to Major Marks's opinion. Wing tells me you are the man for the job, that if anyone can crack this problem you can. *I brought you down here specifically for this*. Now—I would like to know what the hell's happening in Pontoise. We have a lot riding on this, Captain, and we have got to get the show on the road, do I make myself clear?"

"The solution, Colonel, is not difficult," Chimera replied evenly. "But the steps that lead to it are. The solution is simple—it's the getting there that is tedious."

"I need a goddamned answer as quickly as possible."

Still smiling, Chimera said, "And you will have one in due time."

Parker tossed the silver dollar across the blotter and folded his spidery arms in exasperation. Impudent son of a bitch, he thought.

Chimera pushed away from Parker's chair and swung over toward the conference table on the far side of this gloomy office. The table's waxed surface had vanished under a lake of directives, charts, and photographs that represented Pontoise. Through the process of chemistry and timing, the soul of Pontoise had been frozen on photographic paper. Chimera was an architect before Hitler interrupted him; and architects build—they do not destroy—and this is what bothered him.

Before he turned from the table he thought how quickly the dreams that built Pontoise would come to a shattered end and how much that idea filled him with revulsion.

Rowe dropped into the seat next to Sutton at supper that evening.

"You and I," Rowe said, "have a real lulu for a Group Commander."

"Might be, but he's the only one we have, like it or not."

Rowe had flaming red hair and when he removed his cap the top of his head seemed to leap into disorganized fire accented by an infinite amount of freckles. "I know a guy who knows another guy that said Parker's bound for the looney bin. My guy's guy is a doc at Bushy Park, so he ought to know." Bushy Park, just outside of London, was Eighth Army Air Force Headquarters.

"Anybody that flies combat is looney," Sutton said, "including him."

"Including who?"

"Parker—that's who you're talking about, right?"

"Yeah," Rowe said. "Listen," he added quickly, eyeing Sutton's bread pudding desert, "I also got the poop on the big mission."

"What big mission?"

"Are we on the same wave length tonight or are you just jerking my chain? *The big one.*" Rowe leaned over, spelled out the word, whispered each letter: "P-O-N-T-O-I-S-E. We, Captain sir, are going to bomb the shit out of the place."

111

"Who told you that?" asked Sutton, pouring glasses of milk for both of them.

"The same guy who knows the doctor at Bushy Park. Guy flies C-47s down at Keevil."

"C-47 pilot? You mean a bus driver," Sutton said, laughing. "What the hell do bus drivers know about bombing missions?"

"Hey, come on now, don't say that in front of this guy—he's mean and nasty and he's got it all figured why he's flying a bus instead of a fighter. Just the other day we're on a train down to London and he told me, 'You should always fly a big plane. Because if you have an accident in a big plane it's just like that accident happened in another state—the accident will happen *way* out there where it hardly matters. But if you fly a small fucker, like a fighter or an observational type and you have an accident, that accident is going to happen right there in your face.' Can you appreciate that, Jim, or what?"

"What'd he say about the big one?"

"Oh, that. So now you wanna know. Well, you see, he flies generals here and there—mostly here. Yesterday he's down from Great Yarmouth carrying a small short general, and you know how short guys are—they act taller than tall guys, stars or no fucking stars. Anyway, my guy overhears the general, a little loose-lip stuff. The short general is trying to impress another general and tells him that Wing has sent a specialist down here to Bassingbourn to determine just what Pontoise is all about. It seems that Pontoise isn't just another target. I mean it's special, man, really special. My guy even overheard the specialist's name. Take a guess who."

"Your momma."

"Guess again."

Sutton leaned over toward Rowe. "C-H-I-M-E-R-A."

"You get an extra bread pudding."

"So?"

"So what?"

Sutton just looked at Rowe.

"Oh, now you want the particulars."

Sutton nodded.

"It'll cost you."

"Cost me what?"

"That bread pudding."

"Here. Eat it in good health."

"Thanks. They're in Parker's office talking about the mission right now."

There is no thrill to announcing destruction, thought Chimera.

He did not want to face the anxious Irontail, the disquieted Marks wringing his hands over there on the green leather sofa. Chimera could not say he would rather die than make this statement because he valued his life and such a remark would be too dramatic. He would have preferred summary relief, to walk about from the photos, the intelligence reports, and to leave this misery to someone else, perhaps an iron-stomached war lover. And then there was the special knowledge he possessed, that certain bit of information about Pontoise, about Paris, the secret that Chimera held close to his heart. He had studied the photos, listened to the reports from each member of *The Beast*'s crew, and in a while here in this room his secret and what he had just seen and heard would couple perfectly. That connection would begin the destruction of Pontoise.

The office was without a sound.

A truck rumbled past the window, rattled the panes, and the exhaust note roared then dimmed.

The stars were out for the first time this evening, Deneb, Vega, the great constellation Taurus; and they would be shining over Greenwich Village where Chimera lived before the war. Caught there for the moment, white light from the street lamp sparked Chimera's eyes and he put Pontoise down gently and turned, wishing very much that he could hold the secret only a few knew.

Parker looked up at Chimera, his reptilian features sharper, his hands forming a steeple. "Well?"

Marks nudged forward, took a deep breath as if he were about to watch the fat lady turn a triple on the highwire.

"We have a serious situation here," Chimera said, lighting another cigarette then clenching it in his lips.

Parker moved closer to the edge of the desk.

"Pontoise," Chimera said quietly, "is heavily defended for two reasons: the photographs Harrow took show an unusual number of haystacks in the field surrounding the village. Those haystacks are actually hiding the same WGr21 rocket projectile that killed Skolinsky this morning."

"You mean to tell me," Parker said, "that the Germans put all that flak up there for a bunch of rockets?"

"Yes. And no. From Pontoise the rockets are going to be dispersed to various German airfields in the area.

The WGr21 is a new weapon, something the Germans believe can save the war for them. It is Hitler's feeling that these rockets can turn the tide of the war."

"So they have hundreds of those bastards and they're going to attack our bombers with them. Captain, I'm afraid there's more to it than that."

Chimera went on, "We were very fortunate today. Harrow got some unexpected photos of the FW-190 as it was actually firing the rocket."

Marks said, "All right, so we know the Germans have them. A while ago you said there were two reasons that Pontoise is heavily defended. What's the second?"

Chimera shifted his weight, flicked an ash into Parker's ashtray. "On May first, a platoon of Waffen SS troops moved through the suburbs of Paris, and at precisely 1500 hours they were ambushed by a group of French resistance fighters. Three Frenchmen were wounded, two died. The third is still alive."

Marks took in a deep breath, appeared perplexed. "What's the connection?"

"For some time Allied forces have been fed highly classified German information from a member of Hitler's retinue."

"A staff member?" Parker said, surprised.

"No. A non-military person who has been inside Germany since the beginning of the war."

"What does all of this have to do with the rockets and the French underground?" asked Marks.

"Plenty," said Chimera, carefully stubbing out his cigarette and lighting another. "There are only a handful of people who know the identity of the leak inside Hitler's staff. To put aside any question in your mind, I am not one of them. I don't even know if it's

115

male or female."

Parker, fingering his silver dollar, said, "Tell us more about the connection between the spy and the French resistance fighter, Captain."

"The Frenchman knows who the spy is. He is one of several agents throughout Europe with that bit of knowledge. Not only is the spy feeding our agents pieces of information, but often that information is received before the German High Command hears about it. But the Germans aren't stupid—they know what's going on and they've been trying to stop it for some time."

"So," Parker said, "the Frenchman—whom I assume is still a German captive—has an extremely sensitive piece of data in his head and the Germans are trying to pry it loose."

"True," Chimera told them. "After he was captured he was transported to Gestapo Headquarters in Paris. Yesterday, Hitler personally sent SS-General Walther Schellenberg to conduct the interrogation of the prisoner. If the Gestapo had learned the spy's identity Schellenberg would not have been sent in by Hitler. Schellenberg is a deft intelligence officer, a law graduate of Bonn with a strong command of several languages. He's the prize of the SS and SD because of his culture and intelligence and he is undoubtedly on the case because the Germans have a strong suspicion that the Frenchman knows the spy's identity—and they are certain that if they can find out who it is they'll put a stop to the leak."

Marks said, "I'm still not getting the connection between the rockets and the flak and the resistance fighter."

"Okay," Chimera said, patiently looking out the window. "If the resistance fighter breaks down and gives the name of the spy the Germans are going to get something extra for their efforts."

"And that is—?" Parker asked.

"The names of approximately one dozen Allied agents scattered throughout Europe. Agents working for us: Frenchmen, some Americans from Donovan's OSS group, even a couple of Germans. But Schellenberg is a sharp cookie. A short while ago he was given command of all the secret services."

"So?" Parker said.

Chimera turned and faced Parker. "Yesterday afternoon," he said softly, "Schellenberg moved the Frenchman from Gestapo headquarters. We're sure he did that because the underground was about to try and free their man."

"Where'd they move him to?" asked Marks.

"To Pontoise," Chimera replied.

Along the outside walkway they heard the crunch of boots, and beyond it the dull drone of an idling engine.

Parker spoke first. "Then the mission is going to be a diversionary tactic, an opportunity to save the resistance fighter."

"No, it's not," Chimera said.

Parker said, "Then what the hell is it for?"

Chimera turned away from Parker and faced the window and said slowly, "It's a chance for us to kill him!"

A couple of hours after the conference in Parker's office, a number of fliers were in the Officers' Club

117

shooting the bull, playing acey-ducey. Someone had tuned in the BBC and an orchestra was playing a tight arrangement of *One For My Baby, And One More For The Road*. Everyone knew that Skolinsky had been killed on the photo mission. Skolinsky was one of those silent endearing types who kept out of everyone's way and was well liked. He played third base on the Squadron baseball team and he was so good people would come down just to watch him scramble around the infield. A terrific bunter, Skolinsky's pegs from short went as fast as telegrams. So, he was missed, especially by Bush, who spent the day in his barracks, more wounded over the death of his friend than the small bits of steel he took in his own flesh. So Skolinsky was truly missed, and most everyone showed their regrets—except Griffin, who had a dislike for sergeants across the board. There was a distinct feeling of class difference that he was born with, and it would show at the oddest times.

"I'm horny," Griffin said, standing at the bar. "Everytime I come down from a mission I get horny. You'd think the Air Force would take care of this for us fliers. *Griffin is here back from a raid,*" he barked out, *"get him a young wench!"*

"Stop breathing," said Sutton placidly, "that'll get rid of the pain."

Rowe laughed. More than the others in *The Beast*'s crew he was impressed with Griffin's verbal parades; he showed interest, laughed on cue. Griffin played off this, used Rowe at times to show the others that he was an okay Joe after all, that something must be wrong with *them*.

"Flying's the same as oysters," Griffin told them,

118

watching for Rowe's reaction. "They both make me horny. I mean, as soon as we start coming down, I start going up! If you bastards want to keep your copilot in tip-top shape you'll keep coming down more than you go up."

Sutton stood there looking at Griffin. The passive expression on his face must have been upsetting to the boy aviator itching to show everyone at the bar how entertaining and popular he could be. Rowe kept howling with delight at every word. Then, to show how important, how influential and powerful he could be, Griffin told Rowe, loud enough for the others to hear, "When this war's over you can call on me any time if you want a job in aviation." For emphasis he slapped Rowe on the back and Rowe's face ignited with surprise, as if he'd just been handed an unexpected perfect grade from his teacher. Thankful, Rowe kept silent, that look of surprise glued to his puss.

Sutton gave Griffin an unmistakable brush-off. He knew what Roger the Boy Wonder was up to and he turned and talked to Doc Matlin about the "Flying Ace," a 30-ton American Export Airlines plane that, on May 1st, had flown 3,329 non-stop miles from Foynes, Ireland, to New York, in 15 hours and 30 minutes.

"What do I know about flying?" Matlin said despondently. "I'm a doctor. The only thing I know about planes is that they kill and maim people." He took some Scotch, ordered another double and leaned over and said to Sutton, "He's your copilot."

Matlin had his own problems. The main one was being here and not in Seattle where he had a large practice, where his medical opinion was gospel, and where he exercised a considerable amount of muscle among the city's politicians.

Sutton blanched. Matlin had quickly assigned him guilt through association and Sutton felt it was unfair. Maybe, Sutton thought, everyone felt he and Griffin were the best of buddies. Matlin went on in his own negative way, describing in long gloomy detail the injustice he'd been dealt, how life had turned against him, and how his practice was shot to hell because of "this goddamned intrusive war." If Griffin was filled with puffery and prevarication, then Matlin was at the opposite pole—a terribly negative bore who'd bend your ear all evening with his tales of misery and ill fortune. He was a negative man and no one else, according to Matlin's own words, had been more inconvenienced by this war than the doctor from Seattle.

"Doc," Sutton finally announced with a smile after listening to the tale of woe for more than ten minutes, "you are indeed the Busby Berkley of bad news."

Matlin turned, looked at Sutton, a big bewildered expression wrinkling his face. "What the hell's that supposed to mean?"

Sutton said, "It means this. I know a guy down at Martlesham Heath that flew with the 355th, a P-51 fighter jock named Collis, a big likeable, easy-going fella you wouldn't mind passing the time with anywhere. He got hit over the Channel by four Jerries and they blew a hole in his cockpit big enough to slip a pig's ass through, but he still managed to get his ship back—because that's what kind of guy he is. After he crash-landed they pulled him from the wreck and before they had him on a stretcher they discovered he

120

had a foot blown off, and that the only thing that prevented him from bleeding to death was a belt he had tied around his leg. 'Shit,' Collis said, 'I must have lost the bastard dancing last night. But it makes no difference because I hate dancing.' That, my dear doctor, is a *real* goddamned intrusion."

Matlin finally walked out. Sutton expected him to stay on, to defend himself, but he couldn't. No sooner had the door slammed on his exit than Griffin started off about his sexual achievements and Sutton told him to shut up, that he didn't want to hear any more nonsense from anybody. This started a meaningless argument and Rowe was standing between them.

A bottle fell over. Rowe's drink spilled across the bar. There was an intense tussle and both Griffin and Sutton locked like rams fighting for the hill. A punch flew and Sutton's mouth flared with blood. Rowe attempted to break them, referee style, and caught a fist above his eyes and skidded over the bar and crashed into a few hundred dollars' worth of booze. Two trash baskets were tossed over and a mug exploded against the piano. Someone let out a crazy whoop, a joyful sound, and then glasses and bottles and ashtrays smashed against the walls and floor.

Archer Chrisp shouted for a halt and someone gave him the finger. Everyone joined in the disorder, knocking over the magazine rack, the writing tables. Someone took a handful of darts and launched them toward the ceiling and half of them stuck. Chairs were broken and beer bottles crashed through windows with awesome speed. Sutton and Griffin stopped. Through some extraordinary alchemy, their angry clinch subsided into a playful embrace. Chrisp shouted again, less serious this time, and the place took note and went suddenly nightquiet. The orchestra on the BBC played *Spring Will Be A Little Late This Year*. Everyone resumed their original positions again and the chaos vanished. Each man had gone back to what he had been doing, shooting the bull, playing acey-deucy.

"I got my relief," Sutton muttered, as he went off to his room to sleep.

At interrogation late the next morning after a mission *The Beast* flew, Sutton's crew caught a peach-faced captain from Wing Headquarters who wore the world's most unconvincing mustache—something that resembled a dash of eyebrow pencil across his thin upper lip. The captain got off on the wrong foot by asking them what mission that had been for them.

"How do you mean?" asked Tutone, with a little too much aggression in his voice.

"I mean," Peach-Face said in a sing-song tone, "precisely what I asked—how many missions does this make for you?" It sounded as if he was dismissing them as a bunch of green-eared beginners.

This was how it went for the other men, too.

The interrogation was in the briefing hut. A number of small tables were brought in and an interrogating officer sat at each table, a thick stack of reports piled up on each corner, and he took on one crew at a time. When *The Beast*'s turn came the crew huddled around the peachy young captain's table eager to get the job finished, but that quickly changed. Some sat, others stood, still wearing their flying gear with leather jackets unzipped, flying helmets and caps back on their heads.

Tutone was balancing two white mugs of coffee in his hands, which wasn't unusual because he judged a long time ago that that was how long the procedure took—two cups long.

The pink-faced captain appeared very impatient and began tapping his pen on the table, making a loud clicking beat, which stated that he wasn't very pleased with any of the crews' work that morning. None of the interrogators, Kid Kiley later found out, quite believed where the Squadron had been. A ghost mission had been flown, some said; the Squadron couldn't have made such an error; children had better flying sense than that.

The target had been Berlin but nine B-17s, including *The Beast,* had salvoed their ordnance on the synthetic oil plant at Politz, to the north and east of Berlin. The captain would hear no excuses. He wanted a solid reason for bombing an area not designated as a target. Sutton's Squadron—the 368th *Jolly Rogers,* a component of the 45th Bombardment Group (H)—had not reached altitude until eleven minutes before Berlin, the primary target. Berlin turned out to be nine-tenths clouds, and Colonel Parker's navigator immediately radioed course corrections and the Group wheeled around. The sloppy maneuver split the Group, scattered them, and it took nearly ninety seconds for the *Jolly Rogers,* with Chrisp in command, to receive the order for bombs away. No one realized then—including Parker, flying as copilot with Chrisp—that they had bombed Politz, not Berlin. This is what infuriated the young captain.

"What made you think that was Berlin?" he demanded in an insulting manner.

Lamely, Rowe told him, "We figured the colonel's navigator had his head screwed on tight."

Under pressure from the captain, Sutton piled into his crew.

First he told Tutone to keep quiet until spoken to. Tutone, stunned, took a step back and spilled coffee on the Chief's shoulder. Then Sutton demanded that Gibson produce the mission log right there at the table, to prove to the captain that there was no secondary target on the boards, and that they had their coordinates direct from Parker's navigator. They had done what they were ordered to do.

The young captain sat there listening to Sutton as he sailed now into Griffin who hadn't said a peep since the interrogation began. Why, Sutton demanded from Griffin, didn't he make certain that Parker's navigator had them over Berlin, not some unknown oil plant. Sutton's brown eyes were aflame and for the first time since they'd been together he exploded, tearing into each of them as if they were a bunch of undisciplined recruits. The peach-faced captain enjoyed their discontent and let his original tack slip by, relishing the anger boiling among them. It was as if he planned it that way, knowing what happened over Politz and using this moment to antagonize them.

They fell silent and sheepishly answered the captain's ridiculously naive questions, feeling certain that the bastard knew the answers before they got them out.

It took their breath away to see Sutton behave that way and it hurt them. Because above everything—all the fear, the pain, the uncertainty—James Sutton was the one consistent, stable member of their crew. He was their reference point in the blackest of nights, the captain of their ship.

They were through by the lunch hour, looking forward to an unexpected afternoon of sack time and long hours of reflection. The captain was through with them and before they reached the door Sutton broke their silence.

"War is a pain in the ass," he said, brushing past them into the fresh daylight.

TEN

The moon hung crisp against the sparkle of stars and the stars hung profusely like diamond chips tossed against black velvet from the hand of some mystical artist.

Below, where the air was cool black, where the moon and stars allowed some of their light to fall, a pale green Mercedes slid to a halt at the Flight Operations building at an airfield on the outskirts of Pontoise. The driver, an *SS-Feldwebel,* bounced out of the car and opened the rear door. A short, 33-year-old man wearing the uniform of an *SS-Brigadfuhrer*—a general—stepped out. He had a square bony face, a mouth shaped into a frown. He adjusted his peaked cap and walked into the building. The house had been here for nearly a century, the two men waiting in the office for nearly a week.

The office was intimate, furnished as it had been before the Luftwaffe had occupied it nine months ago. A desk, antique chairs, and built-in bookcases surrounded a huge fireplace.

When *SS-Brigadfuhrer* Schellenberg entered, Baerenfaenger and Eder came to attention.

Schellenberg returned their salute. "Please, stand at ease," he said, taking off his cap and placing it near an opened bottle of French wine. Schellenberg smiled. "It is an honor to meet both of you. I have heard much about your achievements." Then he extended his hand to Baerenfaenger. "Congratulations," the SS-General said, "on receiving that," and he pointed to Baerenfaenger's Knight's Cross. "I understand the Fuhrer presented the Diamonds to you personally."

"Jawohl, mein Brigadfuhrer."

"Would you care for some wine?" Eder inquired, walking toward the desk.

"Certainly. I couldn't resist. What is it?"

"A Bordeaux," Eder said, pouring.

"Of course."

Baerenfaenger was cautious. These SS types were egotists who surrounded themselves in an aura of mystery. Army and Air Force people were often looked down upon, as if they were subservient to the whim of the SS, Hitler's private army and secret police. But Schellenberg appeared different, and this was the first time Baerenfaenger had met him. He did not seem as arrogant as most of them. Schellenberg was one of six general officers in the SS that reported to the SS's RHSHA—the Security Department headed by *SS-Obergruppenfuhrer* Reinhard Heydrich until he was assassinated. Afterwards, his office was taken over by Ernst Kaltenbrunner. Schellenberg had made his abilities known quickly, and was in charge of the Ausland SD, the Foreign Intelligence Office responsible for German agents throughout the world.

The men held their glasses high, toasted each other.

"Excellent," Schellenberg said, licking his lips. Schellenberg took a chair near the fireplace and appeared comfortable in the presence of these two accomplished pilots. He stretched his legs, took another sip of wine. "Tell me," he said, gazing at the wine's color, "what do you think of the rocket's performance?"

Baerenfaenger put his glass down on the tray and looked at Schellenberg. "The rocket?"

"You seem surprised," said the general.

"I am. They told us you were coming, but they did not tell us your purpose."

"Ah!" said Schellenberg, tilting his glass again. "I see. But that is often the case. You see, I have come to realize that I can explain my purpose far better than anyone else."

Eder said: "It is unusual for an SS officer of your rank to appear at an airfield such as this, *mein Brigadfuhrer,* and that, I am sure, is what *Major* Baerenfaenger was referring to."

Schellenberg allowed himself to laugh, a short sincere sound. "No offense taken," he said politely, raising his glass. "I often appear at the oddest places, that is part of my occupation."

In 1939 Schellenberg investigated British intelligence in Holland, which was neutral at the time. Posing as a resistance agent, he gained the confidence of three MI5 operatives which led to their kidnap by SS troops. In 1945, he would arrange meetings between *Reichsfuhrer-SS* Heinrich Himmler and Count Bernadotte—the purpose being to arrange an armistice with the Western Allies. When Germany fell in April, Schellenberg was still in Denmark trying to arrange a surrender.

"It is a mixed blessing," Baerenfaenger said, referring to the rocket. Eder agreed. "It comes off quickly, is fairly accurate and most powerful but detracts from the maneuverability of the fighter. If we are engaged and a dogfight ensues while the rockets are attached, we can either fight and perhaps get shot down, or we can fire them and engage the enemy. If we do, then we have lost the rockets."

"I see," said Schellenberg, slipping an ebony cigarette holder from his tunic. His eyelids were half closed and his hands were a dull sheen in the pale desk light.

"You appear surprised, *Brigadfuhrer*," Eder said, crossing to the desk where he had placed his wine glass, his boots clicking on the hard parquet floor as he went. He had made his remark hoping to pull information from Schellenberg, to hear the reason for the presence of a *Brigadfuhrer* here at this airfield in France.

Schellenberg's sapphire eyes widened again and he said: "Not exactly. You see, often we are not told the complete story in Berlin. There are people, politicians, who pronounce everything wonderful. They see things through rose-colored glasses, and that is how they report matters—always positively, without the negative results. Actually, I had my doubts about the rockets, but I never had them confirmed by first-hand experience such as yours." Schellenberg's thoughts seemed to be a confession, humoring himself as he slipped a cigarette into the holder.

Baerenfaenger offered a light, and said matter-of-factly, "The weapon has serious drawbacks, *Herr Brigadfuhrer.*"

For a long moment Schellenberg's fingers were placid, then he raised the glass and the wine sparked crimson. Smoke masked his features against the wash of light. "A large quantity could be effective against a force of American bombers, no? I mean, if hundreds of our fighters possessed them they could be effective, could they not?"

Eder set his glass next to Baerenfaenger's and the crystal chimed. As he regarded Schellenberg's eyes he felt his answer might be the reason for the *Brigadfuhrer's* visit. Why else would he come? A social visit? An absurd thought. "If the rockets are to be used in such a situation," Eder said thoughtfully, "they could be effective, but with your permission, I would make a suggestion."

"I hear experience speaking." Schellenberg was amused.

"I would have a force of German fighters—a separate force than those who would be rocket-equipped—in the air along with a force prepared to use the rockets. If the Americans attack with their fighters, we will then be prepared to engage them. While this is being done, the bombers can be attacked using the rockets."

Schellenberg squinted through a veil of smoke. A calm came over the room and he raised his glass, drained the remaining wine. "I toast both of you." He could see that Eder was inwardly fascinated with the proposed tactic, obviously conceived at this moment.

131

But that was Schellenberg's plan also, his reason for coming here: to have one of these pilots propose the concept, rather than having it forced upon them by a non-Luftwaffe officer—a general from the SS. They would put it into effect with more enthusiasm, he was certain of that.

Schellenberg's short body unfurled from the chair and he padded reflectively across the room and stood there motionless. He turned and faced the pilots, a fine-boned figure in his trim uniform, the silver embroidered oak leaves on the black collar patches glinting in the moon's light. He glanced through the window, over their shoulders. He saw the moon's full, bright shape. Diamond dust and moon beams were embedded in infinite black, showing the way.

Arianne took off her gold bracelet and placed it on the bathroom sink. The *citron*-scented room was porcelain-lined with thick white tiles agleam with steamy chrome. Muted light sparked Arianne's ice-blue eyes and she canted left and studied her figure in the tall mirror: the face was strong, above a regal head and broad shoulders and slender body that tapered into thin ankles, slim feet. The skin was rose-shaded and smooth, the stomach flat and taut, the bone structure refined. Hands on narrow hips, relaxed, Arianne tilted the reflection across the misty glass, studied her slight breasts barbed with crimson nipples; she took them in her hands, cupped them for a long moment, admired them. She slipped her thumbs through the elastic band and drew her silk panties down her svelte legs and stepped away, but kept the image neatly framed in the mirror. Over her head she stretched her slender arms, clasped her hands and tilted far left then far right, watching the muscles tighten . . . relax . . . tighten. Her body was free, lax, but her mind was filled with doubt.

Sutton coughed in the bedroom.

Arianne cocked her head and peeped around the corner.

Shadows danced in the darkness and candle flames fluttered. The filmy curtains were drawn across the wide windows. A broad moonbeam covered the quilted bed where Sutton rested, waiting.

"Are you finished?"

"Are you undressed?" asked Arianne.

"Yes. Are you finished?"

"No, I haven't begun," murmured Arianne, turning.

Sutton had come here around ten o'clock and they had eaten formally in the dining room with its long oak table, peering around the brass candlesticks that they would later carry into the bedroom. Before they dined they had strolled hand in hand into the entwined wisteria, to the balustrade at the garden's edge, while the cook prepared a special meal for Sutton: avocado, tomato and mushrooms with vinaigrette sauce, beef stew Zinfandel, and chocolate roll *mit schlag* for dessert.

What does love mean? wondered Sutton. Had he been so enchanted, so stung by Arianne that he was trapped in the eternal mystery? What was the rapid pulse, the shallow breathing, the riveted gaze that he sensed when he first saw her? Was he being fair to himself, to Arianne, or was he just another lonely pilot overcome by a woman of beauty and grace? *Oh God who the hell knows? There is no clarity, no clear white, no black, just gray.* Maybe someday Sutton would have to say his last farewell, and then what would he sense? Sure, he had been on the losing end before. But would he hurt Arianne with the ice-blue eyes who had brought him tenderly into her life?

Arianne reached down into the marble green tub and turned the gold hot-water tap and the rush of water ceased. Steam shimmered off the water's dark surface and she slowly slipped into the warmth, the water opening her mind. . . .

There was hesitancy in Jim Sutton's eyes, a reticence that Arianne had seen through the candle's glow. If he would leave what would she do? Her pride would be taken back and the lonely world of self-doubt would return with stark silence. Because there are no words to say when a man says he no longer needs you. That is when you must take up your pride and go along with only words you would *like* to say. Each of us must go alone through the night, lighting our own candles as we seek the light. But who would be there for Arianne? When she turned and found no one there to catch her falling who would help her from the edge of the abyss?

The air was still. An owl broke the night silence.

In the dell beyond the balustrade the wind ceased its rustle.

And now the only sound was the rush of Arianne's breathing, the warm water gently lapping her breasts and thighs. She touched her skin, sensed heat, desire. She felt numbed by it—as if that would keep him from her forever. She wanted to force him in; she held herself open, and his hand fluttered there. *Every time you are near* . . . His kisses were gentle, then harsh. Neither spoke but let themselves feel the fire. Even the cooling water did not temper the glow of Arianne's fevered body, silvered by the light's pallid wash. *Whenever I see your smile* . . . Arianne's mouth went slack, her head tilted back. Desire blossomed, unfurled its heavy wings. *Or I hear you say hello* . . . Sitting open now on the tub's edge, offering herself, love taking her higher, beyond clouds and stars where there is no reality. She thrust her hips and felt his mouth where his hand had been long, long moments ago. A hundred nights, a thousand days in this pose would not be sufficient. *Is like the first time.* . . . There was a ferocity in her passion, a manner of anger—anger at herself for loving a flier who knew he was human and not some damned make-believe god.

That same night in a pub called *The Sword and Shield,* Griffin was drunk. He sat forlornly with Gibson and a copilot from Chrisp's ship, a jerk named Namon Reese who had been designated the ugliest flier in the Group. Reese had been half invited, Griffin welcoming him with modest enthusiasm after watching him trying to dock at several tables. For the past several weeks Reese had been going around seeking a copilot's slot, trying to get away from Chrisp, whom he could not tolerate.

"I don't know anybody in his right mind that can fly for that son-of-a-bitch," said Griffin, regretting the remark because it launched Reese into a ten-minute

135

chapter on how much he disliked his aircraft commander.

Moody and subject to lightning changes in temper, Reese was shunned like an unnamed disease. If it were only that, his awful moods, perhaps he could have swung a change in ships a long time ago. But Reese was on his fourth crew—the first three either having been shot down, killed, or captured during an assortment of missions that ranged from the sublime to the insane. Once he had been called away from his B-17 moments before a raid and placed in another ship because the copilot had an appendicitis attack. Inexplicably he had been replaced in his own bomber. Halfway into the mission Reese looked out his side window and saw his plane disintegrate from a direct hit; there were no survivors. Since then the other fliers viewed him as a Jonah, as if the raven from Poe's poem rode his shoulder.

"You can sense what I'm talking about, can't you?" Reese asked them.

Griffin said, "Anyone could." He almost sounded understanding.

"Look," Reese said, splaying his big meaty hands on the table and looking at Griffin, "how about you and I work out a deal? I'll find someone to fly in my seat and you can switch with him. I'll find a ship you like. How about it?"

"No dice."

"Why not? I hear you and Sutton don't hit it off."

"That's none of your damned business."

Reese threw up his hands. "All right, all right, don't get touchy, a guy's gotta look out for himself is all I'm saying."

Gibson interrupted: "Hey, let's talk about something else, okay. Let's talk about dames, that's always pleasant."

"Sure," Reese agreed, smiling, looking at Griffin. "Do you have a girl, Griff, I mean, are you in love or anything?"

"Naw, great pilots only love themselves."

ELEVEN

The next morning it rained. Thick diagonal sheets hit England before sunrise and stormed across *Fortress Europa* with an incessant force, and fat boiling clouds clung to the earth and cut the sun's great light, painting the air a maddening blackish blue. At Pontoise, thunder cracked and drummed the caretaker's roof, and around it the land was a deep, rich, infinite mud. In the Flight Operations Office, Baerenfaenger leaned against the window sill, arms folded, blue eyes peering, searching across the road beyond the rolling, water-drenched fields. Up and down the flightline Focke-Wulfs sat restlessly: sleek shapes muted under the drape of grease-stained tarpaulins.

"A good day for ducks," Baerenfaenger said softly.

Eder was stretched out in an antique chair in the center of the room, hands folded across his chest, a mug of hot coffee sitting on the floor beside the chair. He had been up for two hours—since 0400—checking the new pilots who had arrived a half hour later. Without opening his eyes, he asked: "Do you see the bastard yet?"

Baerenfaenger shook his head, glanced at his wristwatch and impatiently said, "It is 0650. He's twenty minutes off schedule."

"The rain, the mud," Eder said listlessly.

"The rain and the mud are not good excuses for a Luftwaffe *Oberst*." *Oberst* was equivalent to a U.S. colonel.

"Perhaps the bastard broke his ass somewhere, maybe he crushed himself driving into a tree, maybe he is in a ditch right now, dead, or—"

"Maybe his ambition killed him. A lot of officers die that way, and you'd be lucky if it didn't happen to you. You flew with him, no?"

Eder laughed, a snorting sound. "For two weeks during the Battle of Britain. An incompetent fop."

"A Knight's Cross holder," Baerenfaenger noted.

Eder opened his puffy eyes, reached for his coffee. "He received the tin tie because his family is wealthy. They lent Goering a large sum of money back in '33 and Goering in turn arranged for some very profitable military contracts. That's what he got the Knight's Cross for, so don't fool yourself. He is extremely ambitious."

"An ambitious asshole."

"Asshole? God! I didn't know there were assholes in the Luftwaffe, August. You must be sick. Perhaps you need leave, a week on the Riviera with all that beautiful French twat. You could walk up to them and say, 'Excuse me, dear, but as long as I have a face you will always have a place to sit.' Wouldn't you like that? Or

140

maybe Miami or Cuba. Have you been to Miami in America? It is a fine resort."

"No. And neither have you. Listen," said Baerenfaenger studying the field through driving rain, "how should we react to the bastard? Should we kiss his fairy ass or stand up to him?"

"I for one, my friend, do not kiss ass unless it is attached to two well-defined tits." Eder felt for the mug, brought it up to his lips. "Whoever makes this stuff, it still tastes like hog piss." He put it down, thought for a long moment. A shattering thunderclap vibrated the walls, made the glass panes tinkle. When it subsided, Eder said to the ceiling, "Maybe a small amount of ass kissing is in order, but mind you, just a little. You know how well he's hooked to the right places, that he knows the right people—Goering and that crowd. In fact," Eder continued after more thought on the matter, "I would not be surprised if that roly-poly Goering ordered Schellenberg to give the fairy this assignment, just so he would know exactly what was going on. He's a political son of a bitch."

"He's an asshole." Baerenfaenger turned and looked over his shoulder at Eder and grinned. "Maybe we should put in a call to *Luftflotte III* and tell them he's off schedule and recommend a reprimand."

Eder said, "What for?"

"For nothing, to break his balls a little."

"Forget it," said Eder, pushing himself straight up in the chair; he cocked his head back, stretched his neck muscles then looked at his watch. "Do you remember Schellenberg's exact words? What did he say just before he left last night?"

Baerenfaenger's finger squeaked a tight circle on the misty pane. "He said he was sending in *Oberst* Herman von Renz—and the *von* was certainly accented—and that Renz would be overall mission commander for Operation Viking."

". . . And that Renz would relate the details when he arrived this morning," Eder added, standing slowly. He wiped sleep from his eyes, yawned. "Of course when the bastard arrives we'll see what he is made of."

Baerenfaenger nodded, thinking. In the distance, across the deep mist where the road appeared to begin, something moved. "Here he comes."

Through the mist and haze, through the steady pelting rain, Renz appeared in a huge mud-splattered black Mercedes bearing a triangular-shaped gray metal pennant positioned on the left front fender. The white Luftwaffe eagle on the gray background signified that the officer was in uniform and in his official car.

Eder stepped across the window and nervously hummed a quiet, self-composed tune. Baerenfaenger adjusted his tunic, tightened his tie.

Renz's driver, a boyish *Obergefreiter,* dashed through the mud and opened the rear door with a precise motion. He had parked the car against the cobblestone steps so that *Oberst* Renz could jump out, bypassing mud and water. Renz sprinted with the grace of a ballet dancer as the skittish *Obergefreiter* protected his commanding officer under a large, expensive ivory-handled umbrella purchased at some Paris men's shop.

Eder rolled his eyes, shook his head and with Baerenfaenger, turned and faced the door and both stood at a posed but rigid position of attention.

"Greetings!" shouted Renz with a massive, wet grin painted on his effeminate, rosy face.

"Good morning, *Herr Oberst,* and welcome," replied Baerenfaenger with theatrical zeal.

Eder clicked his heels and the crisp sound echoed off the walls like a pistol shot. "Good to see you, *mein Oberst."* The sentence accompanied a quick, short, insincere bow.

"Sorry to be late," said Renz, dismissing the *Obergefreiter* with an abrupt motion of his gloved hand. "Paris room service is atrocious these days. My wake-up call was forty minutes late. Can you believe that!" He unclipped his Luftwaffe belt buckle on his blue-gray leather overcoat.

"Quite understandable, *Oberst,"* said Eder.

"Awful," added Baerenfaenger. "And this weather—"

Renz tossed the coat across the chair where Eder had been slouched a minute ago. "How are things?" he asked, looking at Eder while he pulled off a pair of expensive pigskin gloves, snapping them into his peaked cap and putting it on the desk.

"Excellent, *Herr Oberst,"* said Eder. *"Generalmajor* Schellenberg informed us of your arrival and we anxiously await your orders concerning Operation Viking."

Renz slumped onto the couch. "Please, stand at ease," he told them cheerfully. "Eder, I have kept up with your accomplishments. And you, Baerenfaenger, I read about your singlehanded raid against the American air base in England. Marvelous! How did the Fuhrer strike you when he presented the Diamonds award? Isn't he impressive?"

"Tired," Baerenfaenger said.

"What?"

"The Fuhrer seemed tired."

"Ah, yes, of course, he is overworked, you know. *Reichsmarshal* Goering tells me *der Chef*—that's what the inner circle calls the Fuhrer—is a non-stop worker. He has so much on his mind." Renz's eyes flitted around the room, studied it for a moment while his mind acclimated to the place where these officers worked. Then he said: "So, tell me Eder, how goes it? Have you seen Lecke and that crowd?"

"Lecke, *Herr Oberst,* was killed over a year ago— shot down in flames over northern France." The tone was near condescension, so that Eder could subtly vent some of his disdain.

The sense of Eder's words were noted and Renz's pretty sky-blue eyes squinted with mock pain, as if that brief superficial act would show sincere concern. "He was so young."

"Aren't we all," stated Baerenfaenger with equal rancor.

Eder said, "I can have your breakfast brought in, *Herr Oberst,* so that we may continue talking."

Renz nodded.

He had come here from Paris, through the driving rain, and his self-important manner seemed to over- take this office, to stake a claim to it. His presence, his posture there on the couch, said that this room and this command were his. And it was only his rank and the power bestowed upon him and not his reputation that did this. Renz's manner was learned from back- slapping characteristics found in exclusive clubs that smelled of expensive cologne and money—the sort of dissolute air that accompanies a man of no discernible substance.

Eder leaned his slim body across the desk and pressed a button and an orderly appeared. "Breakfast for *Oberst* Renz, please."

Baerenfaenger lit a cigarette. "We are anxious to hear about the mission, *Herr Oberst*. Could you inform us about what we will be doing, what our target will be? *Generalmajor* Schellenberg gave us an overview."

Renz sat up and leaned over the coffee table. His eyes dulled and his face went serious. "Operation Viking is a responsible undertaking and each of us involved in the operation could make a lasting, historical contribution to the Reich." He reached into his tunic and slipped out a flat silver flask, unscrewed the top, which doubled as a shot holder. He poured *schnapps* to the brim. "I have a cold, or maybe influenza coming on. Care for some? . . . I didn't think so. . . . You are the sort that doesn't resort to this. What does it for you? Women?"

Renz's hand quivered as he took up the silver cup. He was uneasy now, as if some terrible pain troubled his soul. For Renz, ahead was either death or glory. He had charmed his way into a corner and there was only one direction, and toward it he would take his dread and either live or die. He took the liquor down in one gulp then poured another. He spread his hands on either side of the small silver cup, like thin fragile fans that had to be steadied in a nervous breeze. When he spoke he spoke to the table in wispy tones, and the table of course did not stare into him the way Baerenfaenger and Eder did. Renz's words were those of a man who had pushed himself toward the top only for the pomp of office, not because of duty or honor or dedication or belief in a cause. "I have been given overall responsibility for the mission. I report directly to *Reichsmarshal* Goering. At the end of the mission I will have to give a full verbal briefing to our Fuhrer. Whether we succeed or whether we fail, and we cannot fail, do you understand me, there is no room for . . . failure." Renz's eyes dulled again and he took up the cup, this time using both hands, like a priest taking up the wine at Mass. "There are reasons for this mission," Renz continued, "that are too complex to discuss now. But the particulars are these: Operation Viking will be divided into two elements, 'A' and 'B.' Element 'A' will be equipped with the new rockets. This element will consist of thirty-five 190s. Group 'B' will be a mixed group of 109s and 190s, and there will be fifty ships."

"Who will command these groups, *Herr Oberst?*" asked Baerenfaenger.

"You and *Major* Eder—Eder the fighters, and you, Baerenfaenger, the rocket group."

"Is that," Eder said calmly, watching Renz's hands, "the reason we were sent up against the American bomber?"

"Target practice, yes," said Renz, trying to show a smile.

"Herr Oberst," Baerenfaenger said, "with your permission—the rockets are not perfected. They do not lend absolute accuracy and they—"

"I do not wish to hear that!" shouted Renz. *"I did not come here to listen to negativism, is that clear?"*

"But—"

"But nothing! Keep silent unless you have something

146

to add." Renz threw his delicate head back and took down another shot of *schnapps* and licked his lips, sensing the aftertaste. He regained his calm and told them, "The pressure is severe . . . and I would expect you as gentlemen to bear with me . . . to show compassion. . . ."

Thunder vibrated the air and beat the walls. Flashes of lightning ignited the room, bathed their faces a mawkish blue. Rain pelted the panes, trying to kick in the glass and spread its misery here in this gloomy place.

Eder inhaled and looked quickly over at Baerenfaenger standing stone-still near the window. The ash on his cigarette was nearing his fingers. The rain's sound covered their breathing, as if it had come here to accent their doubt.

Renz's hands formed a prayerful pose on his lap and he flopped back onto the couch, exhausted. His jet-black hair, combed straight back from a high forehead, glistened in the wash of light. His gaze drifted from the table's edge without apparent focus and seemed to peer into infinity. Out there, the unreachable answer was too far away to be seen, too distant to calm this restless man who had unwittingly built a trap for himself. It was a trap built on the clay of incompetence, constructed of flimsy ambition and worthless ego; and now it was closing around Renz and not even the *schnapps* would cease its iron-hard jaws from devouring him.

"Are you all right, *Herr Oberst?*" Eder said, taking a step toward Renz.

Renz held up his hand. "I am fine, *Major*. Just a lack

of sleep . . . and this cold. I have been up all night . . . planning. You know how these—"

"Perhaps," interrupted Baerenfaenger, *"Herr Oberst* wishes some rest before we involve ourselves in the particulars of the mission."

"I said no! Didn't you hear me, for God's sake!"

A knock at the door. The orderly appeared with a tray of breakfast rolls, coffee and eggs, but Renz was not in the mood. He watched the orderly pour some coffee into a china cup. When the orderly left, Renz again reached for his flask. Baerenfaenger and Eder stood silently, uneasy, embarrassed. This was the officer *requested* by Herman Goering, the man Hitler had chosen to direct his wonder weapons against the Eighth Air Force, the man who sat now half-drunk wishing he weren't here. For the next few minutes, while Renz sipped his anesthesia and numbed himself from reality, while his hands quivered like ferns, he related the details of Operation Viking. They would go up against the Americans—approximately one hundred fighters—and they would do everything to bring each of them down from the sky.

"There will be some surprises waiting for them, too," Renz told Eder and Baerenfaenger. "Some of our ships will be dropping parachute bombs into the American formations." The parachute bomb he referred to was a little device insidious in the true sense of the word—it was a small bomb attached to a miniature parachute. Dropped from above and ahead of a formation, the parachute bomb drifted down and exploded when rammed by a bomber. The trick was to time the drop so that the bomb reached the altitude of the bombers.

Eder stood away from the desk and bit his lip before

148

he asked his next question. "And who will be commanding our force in the sky?"

Renz looked through the rain-smeared window, stared up at the ceiling.

"I will," he said softly, as if he didn't want the two words heard by anyone—particularly himself.

God help us all, thought Eder.

TWELVE

The May 24th raid on Pontoise was comfortably scheduled for 9 AM. The entire Group buzzed with rumors concerning the mission's objective. There were over three hundred B-17s on the boards, the multitude of Groups and Squadrons intending to meet like the gears in a watch at a point halfway across the English Channel. The plan seemed beautiful on paper but that somehow got screwed up in reality, as if the men flying the raid were the most inept, most unprofessional bunch of aviators in the air. Parker, unusually effervescent, would be leading the raid but would be carrying in his second seat a command pilot named Jack O. Merritt—"two r's and two t's, please"—from Wing who would actually be in command of the mission that morning.

Merritt was slim-necked and sandy-haired with shoulders so narrow that they made his high-cheekboned head seem larger than it was. He stood erect when he walked, barely swinging his long thin arms. Nearly six feet tall, Merritt appeared remarkably healthy and trim for a man approaching forty, trying to look like every divorcee's fantasy of a gigolo who could pleasure their bodies all night long; and he had a set of perfectly aligned white teeth which he generously flashed.

"He looks a little fruity to me," Griffin whispered to Sutton just before the briefing began.

The assembled pilots were called to attention and Parker walked into the briefing hut accompanied by Captain Chimera, Major Marks and Colonel Merritt.

Parker had that authoritarian, serious look on his face—which he seemed to reserve specifically for moments like this. He stood hands on hips and let the fliers settle down before he spoke, looking over the assemblage for a long moment, letting the tension build, because that was his way. A black curtain concealed the route map. Behind Parker, Merritt, Chimera, and Marks stood by waiting their turns to speak.

Parker coughed nervously once then began: "We have a special mission today, an unusual raid against the village of Pontoise." He motioned with his hand and Marks pulled the curtain aside and loud groans escaped the fliers—a few catcalls, a whistling sound like a bomb falling, and someone in the back booed but stopped when Parker tried to spot who it was. "All right, at ease!" said Parker. "This is serious stuff, so listen up." For the next six minutes Parker droned on about Pontoise, the number of ships going up on the raid, and as he spoke he showed his nerves and acted jittery. Parker of course had his moments of weakness

152

and this one showed like a baseball on a bowl of Jell-O. When he was done, he inhaled deeply. He turned and introduced Major Marks, who went down the list: rendezvous points, call signs, the exact coordinates for the target.

Sutton leaned toward Griffin while Marks went on—"This is not going to be a milk run."

Everyone in *The Beast*'s crew felt the agony of anticipation and each of them showed it in his own unique way.

Tutone was more boisterous and excited than usual.

Griffin turned moody and nasty.

The Chief seemed pensive and distant.

Kiley giggled, a kid in the back of a church who couldn't stop laughing.

The rest were a mixture of silence and visible dread.

Sutton wouldn't show anything until the first engine fired before takeoff. Then, like some of the others, he felt like vomiting—a stomach-wrenching sensation that would refrigerate his skin on the hottest of days.

Before the crew assembled in front of *The Beast,* Tutone had spread the grandest rumor of the month, one that would stick forever with each of them. "Hitler," he announced to the crew as they boarded a truck for the apron, "is on an inspection tour and is spending the day in Pontoise. We, gentlemen, are going to have the honor of dropping a few tons of American iron on his head." Someone asked him to verify what he said, what the source was; and his reply, quick as they always were, was typical. "Hey, I got it from a guy who got it from a guy." The ride out to *The Beast* was no less easy but certainly more memorable.

The crew fanned out quickly, collectively nervous, less eager than ever to fly. Because with experience comes the knowledge of what can go wrong: how a single cannon shell placed with the right angle and speed could cut a man in half and spread his body all over the sky, how mechanical failure could kill an entire crew, or how skin exposed to fifty below zero could freeze in a matter of seconds.

Youth had its shield, its naive armor. *The Beast* had taken her men through twelve missions and this one would spell out the number "13," a figure they did not refer to or acknowledge. But it was as if the Angel of Death on silent gossamer wings had brushed each of them with a gentle message of doom.

The Chief was more predisposed to this than the others, having a good and evil spirit for everything they did in the air. That day he climbed into *The Beast* like a hunter going after some dreaded evil, more noxious, more venomous than any other evil confronted before. And of course they all sensed it, wanting to leave the sensation there on the apron where their gear rested. Because it left an imprint, an indelible mark that hung over them, that permeated their skin as if that was required gear on this journey.

Sutton watched Sergeant Holden drop from the forward hatch. There should have been time for each of them to digest their fears, to turn their backs a moment and take stock of where they had been and where they were going. Sutton felt that if he were obliged to watch a crewman die on a Sunday and saw his own death foreshadowed it didn't seem proper to witness another dance of death on Monday and again on Tuesday and

Wednesday and Thursday. If this event should come to a man once, Sutton thought, then he should have some time off to be allowed to scream or cry or run away from the damned thing. If Sutton were older he would need that time. And so here they were going up on their thirteenth raid a few days after Skolinsky had been slaughtered in his glass bubble. There was no margin for pause. Each day would go and the other would come and there would be no time in between—despite the weather, the call-downs, the aborted missions, or the cancellations. There were no days of the week with discernible names. Just one long mission until you were either through it all or dead. And so it went.

"Hey, boss!" shouted Tutone from under *The Beast*'s wing. "We gonna kill some Germans today?"

Sutton turned from Holden long enough to answer back, "Yes, and we're going to end the war." In each man there are rituals, in times of peace, in times of war, and for these two men this was such a ritual.

Griffin was in the right seat and Sutton in the left and they began the complex startup procedure, another set of rituals.

According to the B-17 flight handbook the copilot was the executive officer, the pilot's right-hand man. The copilot had to be familiar with every duty of the pilot; he had to know how to fly the airplane to be able to take over at any time; he had to know the engines, to be proficient in engine operation, and to keep the ship aloft smoothly; he had to have a thorough knowledge of cruise-control data; he was also the engineering officer and had to maintain a complete log of performance data.

Sutton, the airplane commander—more than just a

pilot or a flier—had to be a man capable of leading his men. Sutton was in charge of the ten-man weapon called a *Flying Fortress,* a big bus with a lot of guns and bombs and the capacity to kill or be killed in an instant. But the success of Sutton depended largely on the measure of respect each man gave him. Without it they might have done better walking into a spinning prop.

Now, Sutton checked the fuel transfer valves making sure they were in the "off" position; if they weren't they could have pumped one of the engine tanks dry. Griffin checked the intercooler controls and ascertained they were in the "cold" position. The gyro was uncaged and this was noted. Fuel shutoff switches were "open." The landing gear switch was in neutral and the switch guard was in its proper position. To avoid spot-heating and to allow the outside fire extinguishers to be used properly, Griffin checked the cowl flaps: "Cowl flaps open left; cowl flaps open right and locked." The cowl flap levers were placed in the "locked" position. During takeoff the turbosuperchargers were always turned off because a backfire could blow out the wastegate or severely damage the supercharger.

Sutton told Griffin that Sergeant Holden had found the oil leak.

"But he couldn't repair it, we've got a brand-new engine," Griffin replied, his hands going over the switches and levers.

After the batteries were checked, the inverter switch was turned to "main" and the alarm bell was checked by flipping the switch several times.

The sequence for starting the engines was 1, 2, 3, 4— the Number 1 engine being the outer engine on the port wing. Sutton had watched as each engine was pulled through at least three revolutions. Each of the crewmen took turns at this and this morning Sutton saw Kid Kiley cranking the propellers around. Now the fire extinguisher switch was set to the Number 1 engine in the event of a fire.

"Start Number One," Sutton ordered Griffin.

Griffin energized the engine, at the same time expelling air from the primer with a number of fast strokes that obtained a solid fuel charge. He waited twelve seconds and then Sutton said: "Mesh Number One." Griffin held the starting switch to "start" and moved the mesh switch to "mesh." Simultaneously he primed the engine with strong steady strokes until the engine fired. A cloud of gray smoke plumed from the exhaust stacks and *The Beast* trembled as the engine beat out a steady tempo. The mixture control was moved immediately to "auto-rich." Then, each of the remaining engines was started this way, idling at 1,000 RPM until the oil temperature indicated 40° C.

The rule of thumb for taxiing was *never taxi faster than a ground crewman can walk*. Taxiing accidents happened through carelessness and inattention. With all four engines running Sutton used the outboard engines for turning, while the inboards idled at 500 RPM. Enough friction lock was applied to the throttles to prevent creeping due to the ship's strong vibration. After the engines were turning the vacuum pressure gauge was checked; switches on the command receiver were adjusted; volume controls on the jackboxes were set to maximum output; the selector switch on the filter box was turned to "voice," and the selector switch on the jackbox was placed in "command."

Oil pressure: 75 pounds.

Oil temperature: 70°.

Cylinder head temperature: 170°.

Fuel pressure: 17 pounds.

Tachometers: steady.

Manifold pressure: steady.

Hydraulic pressure: 700 pounds.

Clock: 0855.

"Okay," Sutton said into the radio, "all hatches and doors shut, everybody get their headsets on. We're ready."

Sergeant Holden, standing on the tarmac at his customary position on the left side of the cockpit where Sutton could see him, gave the thumbs up sign. The engines sounded good. Sutton returned Holden's salute and then placed his right hand on the throttles.

The tachs read 1500 RPM and the turbo controls were set to "off." The props were run through to "low RPM" and then back to "high RPM" while Sutton carefully watched the tach for the drop in revolutions—approximately 350. Now he returned the prop controls back to high. An ignition check was made and the fuel and oil pressure and the oil temp and cylinder temp were in the required ranges.

The runup check was completed at the end of the runway and Sutton took his boots off the brakes and eased the ganged throttles forward and *The Beast* roared down the runway gathering speed, yearning for the sky with more enthusiasm than her crew.

The craft achieved 115 miles an hour.

Sutton pulled the stick back slightly, and their ship clipped through the air leaving behind the safety of their home.

They were airborne.

Sutton applied the brakes gently to diminish the speed of the spinning wheels before the gear came up into the wheelwells.

Sutton: "Landing gear up left."

Griffin: "Landing gear up right."

Tutone: "Tailwheel up."

Sutton reduced the power setting when the airspeed indicator read 140, bringing the throttles back to a manifold pressure of 32 inches. Griffin brought the RPM down to 3200.

Both of them went through these procedures more stoically than ever before, and Tutone noted this, feeling the seriousness of his pilots as he never had.

"Hey," Tutone said, "you guys better loosen up, this is going to be a long trip."

"Tutone," Griffin shot back, "I'm not going to have to listen to any of your bumwad stories, am I?"

"But, sir, they relieve the tension."

"The only thing," Griffin said, "that can do that is a soft bed and long woman."

The Squadron was rendezvousing over the English Channel and Griffin kept a lookout for the rest of the bombers.

"What are you so anxious about, Lieutenant?" asked Tutone, slipping two sticks of gum into his mouth and offering some.

Without turning, Griffin said, "This damned mission is too big, there are too many ships and we'll end up all over the sky. They expect us to bomb one small block of some tiny French village. Stupid, the whole thing's stupid."

"I don't think so," Tutone said, mashing the gum down. "The way I see it is, we're part of a solid destructive force, the biggest destructive force in the history of mankind. Our purpose is to destroy, Lieutenant, not to sit on the ground, that's what this bird's designed to do—destroy. They're sending us up here today because they want us to destroy something special. You guys laughed when I told you Hitler could be down there, but I didn't hear anybody else come up with a better reason for this raid. I mean, if you analyze it, what the hell are we up here for? It's got to be something *really* big down there, not just some fart factory." Tutone paused for a moment, noticed they weren't listening. "Did you ever hear the one about the mailman at Christmas time," he asked them, checking the sky.

"Tutone, do me a favor," Griffin said.

"What's that, Lieutenant?"

"Shut the fuck up."

Sutton said, "Tell the joke, Benny."

"Okay. It's Christmas time and this guy leaves for work. His wife kisses him goodbye and she's in the kitchen making coffee when the mailman rings the doorbell. She says, 'Am I glad to see you, come on in.' So the mailman goes in and the woman takes him up to the bedroom and screws his brains out. After they're done, the mailman is lying there smoking a cigarette and he's got this look of amazement on his face. Just then the woman hands the guy a dollar bill. 'Merry Christmas,' she says, which really knocks the guy for a loop. 'I can't figure this out,' the mailman says. 'I knock on your door, we make love, and then you hand me a dollar.' 'There's nothing to figure out,' the woman tells him. 'When my husband left for work this morning I

160

asked him what kind of Christmas bonus to give the mailman and he said, "Ah, fuck 'im, give 'im a dollar.'"

Sutton turned, grinned. "Funny, Benny, very funny."

"Yeah, I know. I was going to save it for Christmas but I couldn't wait that long."

August Baerenfaenger hoisted himself up on the camouflaged wing of his FW-190 and slipped into the cockpit. His crew chief began to fasten the young pilot's shoulder straps.

"You don't look too good today," the crew chief told Baerenfaenger.

"You are too observant, my friend," said Baerenfaenger, pressing his fingers into his gloves. He had been up since five this morning listening to Renz nervously relate the operation's details. It was bad enough that Renz had been assigned to command the operation, but to put him up in the sky with these experienced pilots bordered on madness. The man was obviously not prepared for something as complex as this. He sat in the cockpit of his fighter filled with doubt, on the verge of being sick.

Baerenfaenger's crew chief stopped, took his hands away from the harness. "It is him you are worried about," he said, motioning with his elbow toward Renz's ship sitting in line for takeoff. "He really shouldn't be flying should he, *Major?*"

Baerenfaenger had propped his elbows on the sills of the cockpit and rested his chin on his folded hands. "Excuse me," he said, unsnapping the harness and lifting himself quickly. When he reached Renz's fighter he told the crew chief, "Leave, I wish to talk to the *Oberst.*"

Renz, surprised, looked up. "What—?" Baerenfaenger noted Renz's eyes, that pathetic gleam that came up from the coals of fear.

"Oberst, I do not think you are fit to fly today and I am sure you would agree with that." Baerenfaenger's words came out quickly and looked directly into Renz. "You can claim sickness, a last minute illness, and no one would think you the worse for it, you can tell them you have a fever. But you should not be up in the air. You agree with me, I know you do."

Renz twisted his pretty face around, angled his slim shoulders, his eyes going smaller, the lids masking the anxiety that flared there and he said, "Are you mad? Or has the sun baked your brains? Get back to your aircraft, *Major!"*

"Renz!" shouted Baerenfaenger, dropping the officer's rank. "You do not have the confidence of these men." He pointed to the line of waiting aircraft.

"I am ordering you back into your aircraft!"

A flare tore across the blue sky, a signal to launch the operation. Down the line, thirty-three BMW engines fired up.

Baerenfaenger said, "You can leave the mission to Eder and you can command from the radio."

"I can't," Renz said into his hands, from his bowed head.

For a long time there had been peace here and the air had been a blanket of calm and the sun shone softly, but now the ground quivered and the air cracked, splintered by the shattering roar from the exhaust stacks on the churning BMW engines. Grass scents and flower scents, the rich basic smells of wet earth, were overcome by the bitter-sweet odor of engine oil and burnt gasoline. It came to each of them: the trembling *Oberst* there in the nimble fighter, the Knight's Cross winner standing above asking him to remain away from the sky where he would surely perish. And up and down the line young pilots, poised and tense, throttled their engines, thinning the oil, waiting to be led by someone they could respect.

Renz was distant. His eyes were without focus. His body was hunched and his hands held his arms, a child protecting himself from a ghost that only he could see. "I must go," he said to the floor of the cockpit. "Leave."

It was useless. Baerenfaenger was certain of it as he jumped away and heard Renz's engine explode to life.

Before Baerenfaenger reached his black-nosed fighter he turned once, quickly, and saw Renz lift his arm and wave very slowly.

THIRTEEN

Rowe asked on the radio, "What's the scoop, Tilz?"

He pressed his headset firmly against his ears and waited for a response from Dick Tilzer, deputy lead bombardier in charge of the drop for the task force and the Group, flying now in the nose of Parker's ship.

When Rowe went to work he did it seriously and blocked everything else from his mind. He had everything neatly lined up and ready to go. The initial point was a good ten minutes away—announced a moment ago in sing-song fashion by Gibson as if he were a commercial pilot noting points of interest for his passengers. Before Rowe made his radio call to Tilzer he called up to Sutton on the interphone and asked whether the command set was tuned so he could speak directly to him. "I have to talk straight to him," Rowe said, "so we know what the hell's going on."

It should have been Rowe up there, thought Sutton, because he was the best toggler in the Group. And, of course, no one trusted Parker's people—not that they weren't as good or bad as anyone else, but they kept themselves apart from the rest of the fliers.

"You've got it," Sutton replied.

Rowe and Tilzer chatted back and forth, talking bombardier talk while Rowe checked some of his data for the umpteenth time: drop angle, disk speed, drift. There was no need to tell Sutton how important it was for them to work together because they'd done this numerous times before. Once they reached a holding level it was extremely important for the pilot to keep the aircraft level and steady. A small increase in airspeed or a skid was sufficient to shift the gyro bubble liquid $1°$. Such a tilt could be translated into an error of approximately 440 feet at the point of impact from a hypothetical altitude of 20,000. Once the bomb run was engaged the pilot held the accuracy of the drop in his hands, and Sutton was aware of this.

Sutton gripped the controls, not a grip really but a firm sensitive grasp, and then he looked at Griffin sitting there tense, a wide-eyed young man with his thumb on the call button. Sutton worried about Griffin, worried that he might crack when he needed him the most.

"Target surface pressure?" Rowe said into the radio.

"Two-nine point five-four," Tilzer stated, coming in as clear as a broadcast from Glenn Island Casino.

"Hey, Rowe," Griffin cut in, "don't forget to arm your bombs." His nerves came through on the edge of his voice and Sutton glanced over again, wondering.

"Buzz off, Griffin," Rowe said. "We're on the radio here and I have to finish this."

Sutton told them to knock it off and then Gibson cut

in, "We're almost over the I.P. you guys."

The instrument panel clock read thirteen past ten and they were due at the I.P. at ten fifteen.

Rowe and Tilzer finished their business and Rowe called up to Griffin and asked him to arm the bombs for him, something Griffin had been checked out to do since everyone had been crosschecked on each other's jobs in case they had to fill in.

Griffin said okay and unhooked himself and went back to the bomb bay. "What are the settings?" he asked Rowe.

"The five hundred-pound mothers are one-tenth nose, one-fortieth tail."

"Ah, rajah dodjah," Griffin said, trying to sound confident, jaunty, to show everyone how cool he could be, reminding himself of the old pre-war Roger, the kid he left behind in New York State a thousand years ago—the boy aviator with the blue twinkle in those clear bright eyes. For a moment the thought felt good and warm, but then the familiar sensation vanished with a chilling suddenness when he stared at the face of the bomb.

Griffin's hands were wet with perspiration and a bead trickled down his straight nose, a small pellet of glistening mercury attempting to escape the danger this body could trigger. He didn't want to spend too much time here. He worked fast, a little clumsily. *Suppose this bastard explodes?* Then he stopped and considered the idea. *Who the hell would know, it would happen so fast, a flash, a snap, then. . . .* The bombs looked like fat round black pigs in a freight car staring back at him, holding him guilty for their fate. He saw their little yellow teeth, small fangs, pea-shaped eyes glaring, their bullet-smooth heads ready to poke his face. They grunted and Griffin tilted his head working the fuses, taking deep inhales. Ten of them to fuse and if one of them wasn't handled properly . . .

Then a voice cut in sharp and loud.

"Good morning and welcome to Army Airlines, this is your stewardess, Miss Dappa Snappa. We are now approaching the lovely town of Hoboken, home of famed crooner Frank Sinatra. Please fasten your seatbelts and observe the no-smoking sign. Thaaaank youuuu!" It was Tutone.

Griffin shouted back, "Stick it, Benny!"

But in practice they did fasten their belts because they were approaching the target, and there was the chance of flak and fighter attacks. Either one could knock a man right out of his seat. In the radio compartment and the navigator and bombardier compartments, Bo Baker, Rowe, and Gibson pulled the flak curtains across their windows.

The task force reached the I.P. and the combat boxes broke up into component groups, three to a group, so that each group, following its own designated course to the target, could drop their loads independently on the assigned area.

"This has got to be the most fucked-up mission I've been on," the Chief said, scanning the sky for fighters. "How in hell do they expect all of us to hit one stinking square block in some fart of a village? We sometimes can't even hit the fuckin' country we're over."

"Brilliant observation, son of Sitting Bull," Tutone said from his turret.

"That is going to be one messed-up place," Rowe stated, peering over his Norden bombsight.

Sutton cut in. "I didn't hear anyone ask for any opinions, just keep your yaps shut and your eyes peeled."

There was flak now, delicate puffy clouds of dark gray, shaped like little drugstore cotton balls.

The first crewman in *The Beast* to spot it was Skolinsky's replacement, a 22-year-old Texan named Chili Link, who was so bow-legged he could walk over a barrel without spreading his feet. He told everyone his real name was Oldfield, a family name from his mother's side, and that when he was a kid in grammar school he loved to eat chili so much that he earned the nickname. When he saw the threatening puffs he announced it succinctly: "I see flak." The sky filled, as if an artist had gone berserk dabbing the blue air with smudges of death. There was an odd fascination about them, and unless a burst ignited immediately adjacent to a ship, there was no sound.

"One minute from the target," announced Rowe, his voice no longer calm.

Sutton thought of his father. He had a vision of him on the porch of their house on the airfield, sitting in his rocker, watching the sun going down, standing up when the Western Union boy arrived. *We regret to inform you that your son, Captain James L. Sutton, was killed in action on . . .* The expression on his father's face surprised Sutton, even though he knew his father well. The face showed no sorrow, no discernible shock to the death of his only son. Instead, he sat again on the rocker and placed the telegram on his lap and closed his eyes. . . .

Griffin wanted to tell Sutton he was scared, to spit out his misery and rid himself of the burden, to share it.

He would have preferred to stay here in the bomb bay where he could not see the sky nor the flak nor the fighters, to ride the mission out there with the pigs rather than going back into the cockpit and facing the danger beginning to unfold. With his head resting on the bulkhead, Griffin stared back at the pigs, neatly stacked, about ready to descent. He touched one. The cold metal came through his glove. The damned thing had a spirit, a life! The engines droned, vibrated his hand. Sutton did not call him—but perhaps he did and Griffin didn't hear him. He looked at the bomb bay doors. *It would be so easy to jump out and spend the rest of the war in a prisoner of war camp. A slight muscle action, a little nudge from my legs and I'll be free from this madness, tumbling through the air.* He took his hand away from the bomb. His mouth was dry and he made a fist.

"The bombs are fused," Griffin said into the interphone, and then he turned and made his way to the cockpit and plugged in.

"Flak's gone," Sutton told Griffin, "and it wasn't too damned accurate. Parker's ship has salvoed. Thirty seconds to go." Then someone called out fighters.

"We are too damned late," Eder said aloud, without depressing his microphone button. This was one of the largest American formations he had ever seen. As he sped toward them he estimated that they were extended for at least five miles. The lead ship in the first formation had its bomb bay doors open and Eder saw the five hundred-pounders drifting down through the clear air.

170

Coming down from 18,000 feet, Eder knew that he could not stop to think about how he felt; if he did, he would start with the old routine: perspiration, tight stomach, "jumps" as he called them. He would have time to think about his action up here, to pretend to friends and relatives later that he was always cool and having a good time going up against the American bombers. There was a strange bond between Eder and the American fliers. Often Eder felt that he could talk more easily to them than he could to non-fliers. He had tried to explain this to his mother when he was on leave, but he stopped when he saw the pain of worry across her face. He had accomplished a lot up here in the sky, not down there on the ground where it was so hard to explain what this really was.

Eder depressed his mike button: *Blue Falcon leader to section leaders, pick your target."*

And they answered him in their characteristic way— boss, chief, *Herr* Eder, sir, their affection showing in their lack of formality—but what mattered more was their discipline, the perfection of the formation streaking down from the sun toward the American bombers.

"Klaus calling Eder: I see one with your name on it, chief. Good luck to you."

"And to you, too, good luck also, fat one."

Eder's *Schwarm*—called a "finger four" by Allied pilots—sped toward Colonel Parker's *Fortress,* each pilot knowing that the ship contained the leader of the task force. Eliminating him would not matter much because the Americans were interchangeable with each other, something other armies and air forces could not do. But the big silver ship was Eder's choice and his

171

four-ship formation bore in like hornets going for the nest.

"Hold your fire. . . ."

Last night Eder and twenty of his men had been in the lounge singing and drinking, playing cards, trading stories about war, sex, flying. That was less than twelve hours ago, and here they were strapped into their ships speeding toward the enemy.

"You are on your own, repeat, on your own, fire at will, fire at will."

The plan was this: Eder's group of thirty fighters would be deployed to defend the ships carrying the rockets against American fighters. If there were no fighters, Eder's group would join the attack on the bombers. They would make several "softening" passes, shooting up the formation, hoping for stragglers. Following this, Baerenfaenger's FW-190s would attack, using the 21cm rockets.

Above, Renz circled, acting as overall commander, observing the action. He tilted his fighter over and saw the tiny parachute bombs drifting into the formation. One knocked into a B-17s wing and exploded, a pretty flash of pink light. The crippled *Fort,* caught by ill fortune and modern technology, sank onto its wingless side and dove toward the earth. Flecks of metal and fuselage peppered the air where the flash had been a moment ago and a long cloud of black smoke trailed behind. There were no parachutes and Renz thought of himself trapped by the same centrifugal force. He could sense the crew's agony—trapped, unable to free themselves from their crippled ship—during the long, long time they would experience the horror as they fell. What goes through a man's mind then: is it sheer panic,

172

or does a calm come over him knowing that this is the end? Or does he feel that there is hope until the very last moment?

Renz pulled away from his shallow turn and saw the muzzle flashes on Eder's fighters as they bore in on Colonel Parker's B-17, hating himself for being up here, for not having the will nor the courage to join the fight. Envy filled his heart.

Eder and his wingman converged on Parker's *Fortress* in a scissor pattern—Eder from the left, the wingman from the right—their gunfire shattering the bomber's nose and cutting through the fuselage and wings. The shells hit with a stunning hammer force. Metal bits spun off crazily and dust and smoke caught by the slipstream plumed behind. The Plexiglas nose piece shrouding the bombardier's compartment broke into a cloud of snowy glass, most burst back into the compartment with gale force. Remaining fragments sped along the ship until their energy dissipated and they fell gently to the earth like clear rock candy.

"I'm hit, I'm hit!" Tilzer screamed into his interphone. Then there was a frightening silence and two seconds later a deep airy breathing, the sound of bubbles breaking water in a fish tank. Tilzer, blinded by the impact of speeding glass, slumped over the tangled remains of the Norden bombsight. Less than thirty seconds later he died, sighing something indistinguishable through the bubble caught in his throat.

What happened next was a miracle, one of those indescribable amounts of fortune that only comes to people like Branch Parker. The glass and instruments in his cockpit had vanished in a blizzard, cutting his face. His eyes were saved by his forearm which, at precisely the right moment, he lifted when he spotted Eder's fighters firing their cannons. Despite confusion and shock, Parker remained calm and in control of his torn *Fortress*. Reports from his crew told him that three were dead and two seriously wounded. Merritt, untouched by steel or glass, was in "negative panic"—a total calm before the mind assessed truly what had occurred. Parker ordered him to unhook and survey the damage and help the wounded, but he sat there and stared at his fingers.

"What the hell was that?" Rowe blurted out.

"Parker's been hit," Sutton said.

"He's holding formation though."

"Keep your eyes on the fighters, the bastards are using rockets again," Sutton told his crew.

The rocket attacks came in wave after wave with no span of time between them. Baerenfaenger's group worked in pairs and singly, sweeping in from all angles, blasting their rockets into the formation. If their aim was not one hundred per cent effective, it was a demonstration of determination and courage. Because each wave was met with a blistering return of firepower from the straggling *Forts* as they crossed over Pontoise.

Near Miss, flying alongside *The Beast,* took a rocket in the bomb bay and split in half. One second it was there, the next it was erased from the formation. Tutone described the horrible sight as he swept his turret around firing at the attackers. *"Near Miss* is

174

gone, finished," he stated, too intent to show emotion, like someone announcing the departure of a bus.

The Luftwaffe attacks felt endless, an uncomfortable dream that seemed to have neither beginning nor end, driving through the formation with a tenacity few had experienced before. At any moment the American fliers could see one or several fighters picking at the bombers, probing for weaknesses in the defense. But Parker's ship continued, still leading the Group but too busy to offer commands or instructions.

"*Baker's Bastards* is gone," Kid Kiley told the crew, watching the ship dip over in flames. "She's going straight down . . . burning . . . three chutes . . . she just—Jesus, she just blew apart!"

Rowe knew that Tilzer was dead and he worked silently, thinking about some of the good times they had had joking around London on leave. He'd seen the attack on Parker's ship, saw the nose fragment, so the news was anticlimatic because no one could have survived that. Normally everyone in *The Beast* would have assumed that Rowe's silence meant he was calm and doing his best at his job; but Sutton began to prod him, ask him questions, knowing that he might be disturbed over his friend's death and unable to do his job properly. But Rowe's responses, although clipped, seemed normal.

At the I.P., *The Beast* had gone into Automatic Flight Control Equipment, which meant that Rowe was flying the bomber through the Norden bombsight while Sutton sat with his arms folded watching the fighters. It was one of the things he hated most up here, an ugly helpless sensation, and he was anxious for the bombs to be salvoed and gain control again.

The run from the I.P. to the target took eight minutes, and the fighters from Baerenfaenger's and Eder's groups kept swarming in relentlessly.

About thirty seconds from the target, in a level but grim voice, Rowe said: "Listen, Jim, do me a favor and shut up, I'm doing the best I can. We'll have a good drop, but not if you keep bothering me."

Sutton went silent, feeling Rowe's sorrow for his dead friend.

"Bombs away."

The task force made a wide turn off the target, a big sloppy maneuver with half of the bombers scattered from the other half.

Along the horizon, the ground below, the vast sky above them, the air was clear, free from fighters.

"I think," Tutone said, "that we got the shit kicked out of us." No one offered a reply and their silence was a statement of agreement.

Heading toward the rally point off the turn, Griffin's hands felt an electrical charge in the wheel and he looked quickly toward Sutton. His hands were up in the air and open because he too felt the same sensation.

"Christ's sake," Sutton said, "there's a short somewhere." Above his oxygen mask Sutton's eyes showed his concern, his surprise. "Benny, we've got—"

Gingerly, Griffin touched the wheel again. "It's all right, it's gone."

"We must have taken a hit," Sutton said, his eyes flashing across the instruments.

Then in a tense tight voice, the Chief called out, "The Number 3's smoking, Captain."

The sentence had more power than the jolt Griffin and Sutton had just felt and everyone on that side glanced over at smoking engine.

Tutone had the best vantage point from his target.

"What's it look like?" Sutton asked.

"An engine," Tutone replied. "Everything's normal looking—no oil . . . nothing."

"Still smoking," Tutone said.

Griffin checked the instruments. The manifold pressure on the Number 3 began to dip and there was the possibility that the prop could run away. Without saying anything to Sutton, Griffin moved the mixture control to the "off" position. He cut the booster and pressed the feathering button and closed the cowl flaps.

"It's not feathering," said Tutone. "If you're trying to feather it, it's not—"

"Shut up, Tutone!" Griffin yelled out. "I'm doing the best I can, so give me a break and just shut up."

The prop wouldn't sit still: it palsied and staggered, like a drunk who wouldn't fall down. And now they were afraid that the RPM would wind it up like a windmill until it came loose and slashed through the fuselage. That had happened a week ago to another ship and the gash left a five-foot by seven-inch hole in the fuselage.

"Slowing," Tutone said.

The blades finally slowed so that Tutone could count the revolutions as the prop sliced through the slipstream, and then with a few more twitches it stopped.

There was a lot of work to be done in *The Beast* before she made it home safely and everyone was aware of what was left to do. No one mentioned what might have happened to Parker, because no one had reported sighting him after the big turn off the target.

"Give me more juice," Sutton ordered, and Griffin nudged the throttles. "We need more speed." Because the Number 3 was out, the other engines had to pick up the slack.

The RPM's went up smoothly.

"I'm cutting the fuel to the Number Three," Griffin announced, and then he asked for another report on the feathered engine.

"No smoke."

While Tutone and the Chief handled the valves in the bomb bay transferring the fuel, Griffin watched the gauges and listened to them chatter. Apparently there were holes of all sizes in *The Beast*'s skin—from pea-shaped up to the width of a flapjack.

Suddenly a voice—almost unrecognizable—came over the interphone: "Jim, can you come down a sec, there's something wrong with me." Sutton was busy making the course change and ordered Griffin to unplug and check out the problem.

Baker was sitting at his "desk," arms wrapped around his chest. Griffin thought he must've been hit because his face looked twisted, and he didn't move but continued to stare at the charts on his little table, shaking uncontrollably. "I think I'm going to be sick, Roger, I'm going to vomit. I've never felt like this before on a raid. . . ."

"All right, listen to me. Take off your oxygen mask because you could drown in it, then stick it back on when your through." But before Baker reached up to unclip his mask, Griffin asked him, "Are you hit? Are you wounded, or what?"

"No . . . I . . . I just want to vomit, is all."

"What from? Are you airsick?"

"No."

"Then what the hell's the problem?"

"I'm just afraid."

Sutton overheard the conversation and pressed his mike button and calmly said: "Hey, Baker, listen to me, this is Sutton speaking. I'm going to come back there and kick your ass in if you don't shape up, do you understand? We're all scared and we're all puking our guts up, so knock it off. We've got work to do before we get home safe and sound and I don't want you barfing all over my ship. Do you hear me?"

"Stomach feel better?" asked Griffin, holding Baker's arm.

"Yeah, I guess. You know how it is."

"Sure. Take it easy, okay?" Griffin made his way to the cockpit and slipped into the right-hand seat again. Before he finished buckling up and plugging in he looked out the window. Twenty, maybe thirty miles back, a tall column of smoke rose. Under the beautiful summer morning sky, against the delicate pastures that stretched into the horizon, Pontoise burned.

FOURTEEN

"Parker is up for the Silver Star."

Sutton sat in an open jeep, smoking, listening to Lieutenant Colonel Robilotti, the Group Executive Officer. Griffin, in the passenger's seat, a leg propped up on the fender, cocked his head around and stared at the tall slim Exec with the bushy mustache and ruddy complexion.

"Who told you that?"

"Merritt. He recommended Parker, and Merritt's got pull up at Wing," Robilotti said, glancing across the road. A small group of fatigue-clad enlisted men stood idly around the flower garden near the Group's flagpole smoking and chatting, their conversation barely audible from this distance.

"How many guys do you know have the Silver Star?" Sutton asked Robilotti, who took a couple of seconds to think.

"Three, maybe four."

"All good men, I'll bet," said Griffin.

Robilotti's hands were deep in his pockets and he rocked slowly back and forth on his heels, studying the group of men. "The recommendation was for the Congressional but someone at Wing downgraded it to the Silver Star. What the hell happened up there?"

"You read the reports, didn't you, Colonel."

"Hey, listen, if I believed every goddamned report I'd believe Chicken Little got hit by a piece of sky. You were up there, that's why I'm asking."

Griffin glanced over at Sutton. "The Colonel wants to know what *really* happened," he said.

"Ah, yes, Colonel Robilotti seeks the truth, the light."

Robilotti turned and faced the building a short distance away. "Sergeant Litton!" he shouted out, and before his voice died away Litton ran from the doorway and saluted.

"Yes, sir."

"Those men over there," said Robilotti, "what the hell's going on? They're supposed to be painting the rocks around the garden and the job was supposed to be finished ten minutes ago."

Litton answered, "The rain, sir. The rain held them up a bit."

"My ass. You get over there on the double and tell those men to finish painting those stones and that flagpole in the next five minutes. The damned Germans don't stop the war because of rain."

Litton saluted and ran off.

Robilotti took his cap off and quickly brushed back his black hair in a show of mock desperation then replaced it so that it sat squarely. "Do you know what

I've had to go through to keep this damned place in running condition? This used to be a goddamned potato farm before we got here. Now look at it." He glanced around, savored the general view, and then watched Litton talking to the group of painters. When they spotted Robilotti they went for their buckets and brushes and began slopping paint on the rocks. "Do a neat job!" shouted Robilotti.

Sutton said, "Colonel Parker was the first ship in the formation. He got nailed by a pack of fighters that came out of the sun. A classic pincer movement—one from the left, one from the right."

"Apparently," Griffin added, "he has sex with Lady Luck."

"Nevertheless," Robilotti said, "Wing is nominating him for the Star."

"Wendell Wilkie got nominated for President," Sutton told them, sitting up straight.

Robilotti looked up at the gray mass of clouds, and he said: "Yesterday sunshine, today bullshit."

Griffin asked about the citation. "What's it say?"

"I didn't see it," Robilotti said.

"But you heard."

"What difference does it make."

"Because," Sutton said quickly, "you're the one asking what he did up there. We know."

"Then tell me."

"I just did," said Griffin, stepping out of the jeep.

Litton ran past, saluted Robilotti again and disappeared into Parker's office.

"You only told me about Parker getting hit. What happened after that?"

"We didn't see anything," Sutton told the Exec while

he field-stripped his cigarette. "We only saw him get hit. After, there was confusion and when we turned off the target Parker was off the radio trying to keep his ship afloat. The rest you know—at least as much as we do."

"They're making him into some kind of hero," Robilotti said casually, eyeing the painters again, bent over now, carefully painting the big stones with short neat strokes; the sight made Robilotti feel good, gave him a sense of pride.

Griffin glanced at his watch: two minutes before ten and the appointment was for 1000 hours. Robilotti let out a sigh, inhaled the fresh air. Sutton asked him:

"What's Parker calling us in for? He's not chewing us out again, is he?"

"Hell, no." Robilotti smiled, a mouthful of perfect teeth. "You gents are in for a treat—and don't ask me what it is. The colonel will give you all the details."

Griffin zipped up his leather flight jacket. A damp wind had come along, the front edge of a dreary English storm. He said, "It comes as a surprise that Parker's up for the Silver Star. You don't suppose," he added thoughtfully, without looking at them, "that it has to do with a promotion to brigadier, do you?"

Robilotti shook his head and showed his teeth again. He was aware of Parker and his ambition to make general before his fortieth birthday. Between Griffin's words was a direct inference and Robilotti picked it up quickly. "So, he's friendly with Merritt and Merritt is friendly with the people that ordain generals, what does that mean? Besides, Parker knows someone in the Pentagon."

"Look," Sutton said, "sixty per cent of the task force

missed the target and bombed the whole damned village. Sure the objective was hit—and, by the way, everyone knows what the *real* objective was. But in effect, Colonel, what we did was throw out the baby with the wash. We hit the objective but destroyed the village. Now, if someone is going to tell me that the task force commander, Colonel Parker, should be awarded a Silver Star for that, then I'd have to tell them that that's a bunch of hooey."

"What are you trying to say, Captain?"

"Colonel, what I'm saying is—under those circumstances everyone on the raid should be awarded the Silver Star.

Robilotti appeared perplexed and his eyebrows furrowed neatly across his tanned forehead and he asked, "Why?"

"For surviving," Sutton replied quickly.

At Pontoise Airfield, 0959 hours, a black Mercedes pulled to a halt in front of the Operations office and a short roundish man with stooped shoulders and rimless glasses stepped from the rear and hurriedly walked into the office. The man wore an SS tunic with the insignia of an *SS-Oberfuhrer*—which had no equivalent rank in the U.S. Army, but lay between the ranks of a full American colonel and a brigadier general. The *Oberfuhrer* wore bloused gray pants over a pair of laced combat boots and walked with a distinct limp. He was a humorless man with deep-set black eyes that could have been stolen from a hawk who hated everything in the forest. The door swung open and August Baerenfaenger appeared from the shadows of the vestibule.

"I am *Major* Baerenfaenger, *Herr Oberfuhrer.*"

"Is he here, *Major?*" the *Oberfuhrer* asked curtly.

"He is." Baerenfaenger motioned to the door of the office behind the *Oberfuhrer.*

"What is his condition? Drunk as usual, I am certain."

"Perhaps."

"I have heard about you and your achievements, *Major,*" the *Oberfuhrer* said, glancing at Baerenfaenger's Knight's Cross, "but I didn't know you were also a man of understatement."

The *Oberfuhrer* had a chubby face derived from too many sweets—he preferred chocolate cake and candy—and too much "seat time." He was here on this special mission, the end of a short chain that led directly to Adolf Hitler, a chain that began with the *Oberfuhrer's* superior: *SS-Obergruppenfuhrer* Muller, head of the Investigation of Opposition Department (the Gestapo). Muller in turn reported directly to Ernst Kaltenbrunner who had been instructed by Himmler to send the *Oberfuhrer* here. But Himmler's request was not original. Yesterday, after Operation Viking, he was given an order by Hitler that ultimately led to the *Oberfuhrer's* hasty departure for this desolate airfield.

Baerenfaenger took the *Oberfuhrer's* raincoat. "Do you wish anything?"

"Certainly—two guards: one posted at the door to this office and one at the entrance to this building. That will be all."

Renz was slumped behind the desk, his tunic opened at the collar, and he did not look up when the *Oberfuhrer* entered the room.

"*Oberst* Renz, I am *SS-Oberfuhrer* Jackel." Renz remained still and gazed at the ceiling, cigarette smoke spiraling from an ashtray, a glass of *schnapps* on the blotter. "I see," Jackel said tersely, "that *Luftwaffe* officers are not taught the requisites of military etiquette, but I shall pay it no mind. I am here, rather, on a more serious mission and—"

"I never liked your uniforms. I mean, black and silver with a skull and crossbones—how damned pompous."

Jackel reached into a leather briefcase, removed a single sheet of paper. "I have been sent here, as I am sure you are aware—by an order from the Fuhrer himself. I am therefore an emissary of our Fuhrer and I speak in his name, a task that I take quite seriously, and that you, as an officer of the Third Reich, should take also. But, *Oberst* Renz, as unpleasant as this task might seem, it still is something that must be done."

"You are a very pedantic man, *Oberfuhrer*. Please bear me no further pain and get to the damned point."

The *Oberfuhrer* adjusted his glasses and read from the letter:

"'*To Oberst Eberhard Renz from* Generalfeldmarshal *Goering: on this date you will surrender all rank and privileges and will place yourself in the remand of SS-Oberfuhrer Jackel for transport to the Supervisory Board of the Penitentiary in Brandenburg-Gorden. There you will remain in custody of the* Polizeeiprasidium *Berlin as conveying authority, and you will remain so until further notification.'*"

"Life imprisonment," Renz said rather dryly, reaching for his cigarette and the *schnapps*. "What, may I ask," he said after inhaling deeply and sipping his drink, "is the *formal* charge? I mean, these things can be so cloudy. Is it cowardice?"

Jackel considered the question for a second then stated the precise charge registered: "Dereliction of duty. By the way, there are two SS guards waiting beside my car and I have two others posted outside this office. Therefore—"

"Escape!" shouted Renz, almost joyfully, feeling the effect of the liquor. "Me! Ha! That my dear *Oberfuhrer* is part of the Renz mystique. Tell me," he said, "was Goering really behind this? I suspect that he was. Pressure from the Fuhrer, and then the accusing finger at me. As a matter of fact I think you are in the presence of a scapegoat, no? After all," said Renz, sitting up board-straight, "the mission was not *that* dismal."

Rapidly, Jackel said, "Twenty-three German pilots killed, six wounded. Thirty-six German aircraft lost. The Americans reached their objective, bombed it effectively, and the Frenchman is dead. A *disaster,* Renz, a *disaster."* He almost spit the word out.

Renz slammed his fist on the desk. "There were over thirty B-17s downed. Half the rockets found their marks."

Jackel was silent. Lamplight reflected off his thick flat eyeglasses and hid his eyes.

"And," Renz went on, "the Frenchman's death—I am sure that has everything to do with my arrest, correct?"

"You fool! The Frenchman was killed and he was supposed to have been preserved."

"That is my point, you asshole! I did not kill the son-of-a-bitch, the Americans did. You see, this is something that a non-flier cannot comprehend, you do not comprehend the mind of Goering, the only thing you know is that damned ridiculous black and silver uniform."

Calmly, Jackel said, "I am not following your logic, Renz. You drink too much, you smoke too much. You have been under pressure and you are now under arrest. Time to go," he said, checking his watch against the one on the wall.

Renz slumped back into the chair. "Goering felt that the Americans would only bomb the house where the Frenchman was and Schellenberg agreed. By the time they were certain of the raid by the Americans it was too late to move the Frenchman away without risking his capture elsewhere. So Goering had him moved to the railway station. He felt the Americans would only bomb that one square block; he was thinking like a German, not an American. He did not dream, of course, that in their sloppy way that they would bomb the piss out of the whole damned village just to get that single man."

Renz stood, raised his shot glass. "Three fucking cheers for the American bastards, God love their souls. They shall inherit all of war-ravaged Europe. They shall soon own Germany, and may their forces bomb the crap out of the damned Russians. Hear, hear!" He brought the shot glass down gently and placed it on the precise spot where it had been. "Don't you see— Goering screwed up and I am taking the blame. It is like a soccer game—from Hitler to Goering to Renz, a flier without influence." With a quick tug, Renz pulled his tunic straight and angled his peaked cap the way he preferred. "As for me," he said, turning the corner of the desk smartly, "the war is over. But that asshole

Goering will someday have to face Hitler, and that, my dear Jackel, is a fate much worse than death. Shall we go?"

"I thought the world exploded."

Parker wore two bandages, one on each cheek like two symmetrical strokes of white war paint; and his bloodshot eyes were watery balls accented by black and blue circles around vermillion sockets. His eyelids showed a steady flicker as he turned and watched Sutton and Griffin enter his office. He stood behind his desk, hands in his pockets, canted toward the window where he'd been watching the enlisted men painting the rocks white. If an artist painted a horror mask for Halloween, Parker would have been an excellent model. Sutton and Griffin stood before the desk, silent out of respect for the colonel but a little shocked at his appearance. They listened attentively as he spoke.

"Everything turned white, the color of paper, and then bright red as if someone had splattered tomatoes over my eyes. In the first second or two I thought that one of the fighters had flown into us, that we had collided. And I thought that death wasn't that terrible after all, that there was no pain to it—just red and white. Everything was all right until I opened my damned eyes and discovered that the glass on the instruments had vanished and one of the windshield panels had disintegrated." As he spoke, Parker touched one of the bandages, a little exploratory gesture. "It looks a lot worse than it is. Please have a seat."

Sutton thought Parker seemed gentle. Maybe the

190

proximity of death had softened Parker; maybe it had taught him the value of life.

In a subdued voice, Sutton said, "Colonel Robilotti just told us that you've been nominated for the Silver Star."

"Yes, can you imagine that!" Parker said, grinning. "Me, old Branch Parker up for the Silver Star. I couldn't believe it, not in a million years. I mean, I went up there like all the rest of our boys and, *bango,* a shot at the Silver Star."

"Yes, well, those things do happen," said Sutton, taking a seat.

Parker thought he heard a condescending note in Sutton's voice. "Hey, listen," he said joyfully, "this calls for a drink." He pulled out a bottle of Johnny Walker Black from the bottom drawer. "Come on now, how 'bout a pop for you guys."

Sutton and Griffin nodded and they watched Parker pour two hefty shots into crystal tumblers that sparked blue and red in the sunlight. They hoisted their glasses, clicked them, and drank.

"Excellent," Sutton said, picking up the bottle and reading the label aloud while the booze warmed his throat: "'*By appointment to His Majesty the King. Highest Awards: Sydney, 1880; Melbourne, 1881; Adelaide, 1887. Same quality throughout the world.*' And look"—he held the bottle higher and showed them—"here's old Johnny Walker himself with his white riding britches and black boots and his red-tailed jacket and yellow high hat. You know"—he put the bottle down and stared at the label—"I never can tell if Johnny Walker is coming or going." Sutton leaned over for a closer look. "Do you have any thoughts on that, Colonel?"

"Man cannot escape his destiny," Parker said. "And it would seem to me that Johnny Walker's is to be forever locked on that label." Parker smiled. But beyond the watery bloodshot eyes there was a distinct look—Parker knew what Sutton was getting at, and he wasn't going to let the bastard get his goat over a character on a booze label.

Sutton took in the look for a few seconds, took another sip and brushed his lips. "I think it's an interesting label, a metaphor. But, of course, once one has drunk the contents one's judgment changes drastically."

"To what?" asked Parker.

"Well, Colonel, you know how it is—your perspective changes and you take on a different feeling for Walker there."

"And what is yours, Captain?" Parker's smile was fading.

"I would have to pick both—Walker is arriving and departing."

"Interesting. Perhaps you could elaborate."

"Certainly. As I've said, the label is a metaphor."

"For what?"

"Well, I don't think you asked us here to praise you or to congratulate you. I mean, I don't think you called us here to discuss the Silver Star."

"Get to the point."

"I believe you called us here to tell us that we're leaving—like Johnny Walker, we're coming and going at the same time."

Parker knew when he was patronized, particularly by this upstart captain who didn't shake his hand and offer him good luck. Parker laughed though, a good deep laugh, the kind actors make. "You came in that door and you'll be leaving through that door," he said. "Does that explain the mystery of Johnny Walker?"

Sutton resisted the temptation to laugh, but he joined in. "It seems," he said to Parker, "that I am not the only flier with an imagination."

"Sometimes," Parker said evenly, turning and looking through the window and pointing with his thumb, "I wish I were one of those guys without responsibility, just doing one simple task." Then with an uncharacteristic gesture he scooped up the bottle and peered at the label. "The responsibility of rank makes me feel as if I don't know whether I'm coming or going sometimes." It was meant as a joke but it didn't come off, and even Griffin failed to see the humor because it sounded so damned self-serving.

Sutton said, "The burden of rank often has its rewards, Colonel."

"Such as?"

"Achievement, a notion of accomplishment, the capacity to acquire and delegate authority. By the way, Colonel," Sutton said lighting a cigarette, "why'd you call us here this morning?"

Parker gave off another loud laugh, this one very genuine.

"Because," he said, "you boys are flying off to Russia in two days."

It was the last laugh of the meeting.

FIFTEEN

Poltava. Intriguing, enigmatic, unknown.

Gibson pulled the map from a fat briefcase and spread it on the hood of a jeep below *The Beast*. The crew huddled around like a bunch of first graders listening with eagerness to a geography lesson. Sutton used a stubby pencil as a pointer and began to unravel the mystery.

Curiosity, apprehension, and a dash of wonder marked their faces. This crew had been through a lot together and they had worked in the air like a gearbox; they had lost one of the family on a recent mission. Equally, they had shared the misery of attack, the elation of victory, only to return to it again and again to prove, to themselves, who and what they were.

They would fly to a small Russian town, another spot unknown but as dangerous as the renowned cities of Paris or Berlin. Death was death whether it was to be met in the halls of victory or the backlots of defeat.

Sutton stabbed Poltava with the dull tip of a government-issue pencil. "This is it," he said, dragging the words out. "This is where we will be this evening."

"Kind of sudden, isn't it, Captain?" Kid Kiley said for the rest of the crew, staring at the spot where the pencil rested.

"Sudden or not, we leave in one hour."

Poltava was over seven hundred miles east of the Russian-Polish border, approximately four hundred miles north of the Black Sea. Flight time from England would be twelve long hours. "Enough time," Griffin said, "to listen to three hundred Benny Tutone jokes." For the unusually long non-stop flight Sergeant Holden fit *The Beast*'s bomb bay with a fuel tank, and while they finished off last-minute preparations Sutton continued briefing his crew, gesturing with the pencil.

Divided into three combat wing formations, one hundred and sixty-three B-17s with preselected crews would fly to Poltava. The suddenness referred to by Kid Kiley was due to the secrecy that had been in effect from the early planning stage. If the crews were told weeks, even days before, word would have leaked and the mission jeopardized. To give the mission a double-bladed effect a synthetic oil plant fifty miles south of Berlin would be bombed on the way to Poltava. After the bombing raid the *Fortresses* would be met by four squadrons of P-51 *Mustang* fighters that would accompany them into a Russia.

"This is history in the making," Tutone said in *The Beast*'s cockpit, "something that none of us will ever forget." He stowed his gear as he spoke, an unusual tone of elation in his voice, as if he were leaving on a lovers' weekend. "I don't know if you understand what this means," he said to Griffin. "I mean, we are trailblazers, that's what we are. We can tell our grandchildren we were in Russia."

"If we live that long, Tutone, if we live that long. You keep forgetting that," Griffin said, glancing down his checklist. When he looked up he saw T.R. wheeling up on a bicycle.

T.R. took her hat off and let the breeze lift her silky hair. She smiled as Sutton approached. "I thought I'd come by," she said, "to give you a big sendoff—you know, the kind you see in the movies—but, God, that's hard to do. I had a few words to leave with you but for some reason I don't think I'm going to get them out the way I wrote them in my head." Her voice went still and she tilted her head back and stared into Sutton's brown eyes, looking beyond them, wondering what he thought.

Sutton said, "I've thought a lot about what we did and said there at Southport. I want to tell you how I feel because—"

"There's no need, Jim. I don't want you to think that I have to cling to you. I know you're a free spirit, that you need room . . . but you tossed me pretty high and I don't think I've come down yet. I mean, no one has ever done that to me before. I think what I'm trying to say is . . . it's hard to put all your chips on love when all we know is how to keep moving forward toward tomorrow. Nothing lasts forever. The odds are always against that, aren't they?"

Sutton took T.R.'s hand. He hated goodbyes—

because once you said goodbye you might never say hello again.

"Love lies, I've learned that," T.R. said. "It comes dressed in deception, accommodating your feelings to suit the need of the moment. And most of the time it's unreal—not meant for eternity, but for the moment. So, I don't want to put any pressure on you, Jim. In the end I just want you to know that when you're down . . . when you can't get your wheels up, I'm your friend. And that is really the most honest, lasting gift I can give. I'm your friend, at least for now. . . . Who knows about tomorrow."

"I want to kiss you."

T.R. looked down at their hands then glanced over Sutton's shoulder. "You have an audience and a big airplane staring at you."

"Then this is for the price of admission."

The kiss was blinding. From the cockpit, from the waist gun position, from Tutone's upper turret, it was an odd vision—a moment of sentimentality silhouetted against warfare, a man and a woman totally disregarding the unwritten code of men. Their stupid rule stated bluntly that men should not show their emotions, that they could not cry or kiss openly.

T.R. did not know if she would see Sutton again. She was leaving England for the States and there was no guarantee that she would return again. They didn't say goodbye and T.R. pedaled away not looking back, wondering if she would ever see Jim Sutton alive again.

At 32,000 feet the Junkers Ju 88 had begun to spew two white feathery trails in the thin frigid air. The exhaust from the 1700-horsepower BMW radial engines contained fuel gases, carbon monoxide, and water vapor. When it spit from the hot exhaust stacks and hit the cold upper air, it formed cloudlike condensation and streams of water crystals. The crystals melted slowly in the chilled air, leaving faint chalky lines. The pilot watched this in his mirrors and nudged the control column forward. The dark green fighter responded with a shallow dive. The altimeter needle rotated slowly backward and as suddenly as it began, the train vanished. Only at that precise altitude with that precise temperature did the condensation trails form.

The pilot pulled back and the ship leveled off. This was his maximum height for safety. No enemy could pounce on him from above without leaving the same telltale trail he had just left. The pilot's only concern now was the air below. He yawned and for the tenth time checked his instruments, the fuel levels, the pad and pencil strapped to his thigh. The cockpit was too warm and he lowered the temperature. Few men had seen the world like this, a majestic view from this height—brownish, flecked with clouds shaped like whipped cream that spilled into the horizon perhaps 200 miles away. Above, the sky was a clear vivid blue, richer and deeper than the perception from lower altitudes. The pilot checked the chronometer in the instrument panel.

He had been airborne for forty-seven minutes and, according to his mission order, would patrol this area for another fifty minutes before beginning his descent. The chronometer read almost 3 PM. Before dinner he would be seated behind the chessboard playing another engrossing game with the new officer from Berlin. The pilot looked forward to the challenge. Like all veteran fighter pilots he had survived by continually scrutinizing the sky, never resting his eyes for one minute. In less than one second he could miss the speck that could blow him from the sky. As he sat there his head swiveled around and up. In the mirror he saw his radar operator hunched over the screen.

Two hundred miles away in the *Luftflotte* radio monitoring and interception department, a young *unteroffizer* ripped a sheet of teleprint paper off a machine and read the cryptic message.

+JT   21.5.1944

MTR PRM I
SARNEJEOSPAR EAST
LUFTFLOTTE 4, GOG. UNSAFU

   USAAF with approx 150 B-17s expected target east of Kiev

The *unteroffizer* folded the sheet and carried it to a wireless operator in the next room. The message was a general alert to be sent out immediately to all land and air forces along the expected route of the American bombers. The radio operator went quickly to work, transmitting the encyphered message. A few moments later the pilot in the Ju 88 received a single coded word in his headset:

Mountain top.

The pilot quickly gulped the remains of the coffee and called out to his radar operator, "Did you hear that? American bombers in our vicinity. Do you have anything?" Earlier, the pilot had been briefed: he was only to track the Americans and report their course.

The radar operator, crouched close to his radar screen, replied in the negative. "The ground echo at this altitude wipes out the elevation blip. Perhaps you should wing over for a closer look."

The pilot rolled the small control wheel and the flaps closed. He gently pushed the yellow throttle knobs and the BMW engines tapered from baritone to tenor. They were powerful engines but the heavy radar aerials poking from the ship's nose made the fighter a little clumsy. It took a different power setting just to maintain level flight. The ship dipped and made a wide sweeping arc, gaining speed but losing altitude. *"There!"* shouted the pilot into his microphone, staring amazed at the American formation peacefully droning along six thousand feet below. He called out to the radar operator and ordered him to note the coordinates and send them to the operations officers at *Luftflotte* headquarters.

SIXTEEN

At Poltava, four hours later, *The Beast* came to a halt. After twelve hours aloft the silence seemed louder than the roar of the engines.

A stream of military vehicles filled with uniformed Russian airmen and army personnel gathered around the bomber as Sutton's crew slowly prepared to leave. Muscles were sore and it was difficult to move. From the cockpit, Sutton glanced down at the waiting crowd.

In the moonlight a long line of P-39 *King Cobras* and Russian-built Lavochkin LA-7s sat dormant. This was a large airbase but the facilities appeared antiquated and careworn.

Sutton was the last man to leave *The Beast*. He dropped from the forward hatch and joined his waiting crew under the nose and stared back at the group of Russians. After a long moment of silence, Sutton stepped forward and saluted the group.

"Hello. We are Americans."

A short man wearing the insignia of a Russian Air Force captain stepped forward abruptly. He was hatless and his black crew cut shone in the dull night light. "Hello," he said in decent enough English, "welcome to Poltava. We are Russian . . . we are fliers like you." After a sharp salute he took a step closer and extended his hand to Sutton. "Welcome," he said, grinning now. "I would like to introduce myself. I am Captain Yurasov. I am Executive Officer here at Poltava."

Sutton returned the smile. "I'm Captain Sutton, and this is Lieutenant Griffin, my copilot." As Sutton introduced each crewman, Yurasov shook their hands, maintaining his broad grin. In the background an assortment of Russian pilots, staff nurses, and maintenance people looked on, some tipping on their toes for a better look at the Americans in the beautiful leather flying gear.

After the introductions, Yurasov took three steps back and stood at attention, prepared now to make a formal announcement. "I would like to introduce our commanding officer, Colonel Vadim Zhuk, a hero of the People's Air Force." Suddenly the crowd parted, halved by Zhuk's rapid entrance through the center of the hushed group.

Zhuk was thick-chested and sandy-haired, with shoulders so smoothly joined to his neck that it seemed he had no neck at all. His head was so large that it made his chest seem smaller than it was—a wide, square head that he angled to the side and up when he walked, swinging his full-muscled arms as if he would smash through anything that came in his way. Over six feet tall, Zhuk had a set of aggressive berry-shaped, honey-colored eyes that you'd see on a nasty bear. As Zhuk waddled toward Sutton his eyes seldom glanced to the sides, but remained fixed straight ahead, with their fiery glint suggesting a tone of absolute determination. When he spoke he uttered a grunt, the sound carrying through the cool air with a deep basso tone, as if fashioned from pure inner strength that complemented the brutish appearance. Zhuk could have been mistaken for a football player or a wrestler, a man with little intelligence. In that first instant when Zhuk walked through the crowd, Tutone thought of a nickname for the Russian colonel that would stick until they left Poltava: he called him "Roadblock." No one in *The Beast*'s crew questioned the origin of Tutone's hastily coined name and they understood why it came to be.

Zhuk halted in front of Sutton and mumbled something in Russian to Yurasov, who translated: "Colonel Zhuk wishes to know who you are and where your mission originated."

"My name is James Sutton, captain in the United States Army Air Force. Twelve hours ago we left our airbase in England."

In English, Zhuk asked, "You are not General?"

"No, sir. I am a captain—an aircraft commander."

"Where general?"

"There is no general, sir. We are commanded by a colonel, a man equal to your rank."

Again Zhuk spoke to Yurasov who translated— "Colonel Zhuk wishes to know where your colonel is and why he was not first to land."

"Colonel Parker's aircraft experienced an engine failure and he fell back. He should be landing soon."

Yurasov repeated what Sutton had told him.

Zhuk smiled, and his honey-colored eyes shone like polished topaz; he extended his meaty hand and Sutton thought Zhuk would break the bones in his fingers.

Slowly, Zhuk said, "You are first American bomber here at Poltava. Congratulation." His big bearish head was angled now so that he faced Yurasov and spoke a paragraph or two in Russian.

Tutone whispered to Kid Kiley, "How'd you like to have him get you out of bed for a mission?"

Yurasov gave the translation. "Colonel Zhuk says that because you are the first Americans here he has something special for you. He says this is an historical moment. He wishes to extend a gesture of friendship, and he says he likes you very much. He likes all Americans. He wishes to show his appreciation for being here to help Russian people fight the German donkeys. Because of this—"

Zhuk interrupted. "I am ace . . . fighter ace. I destroyed fifteen German planes." He grinned and lifted his big arm and pointed to a *King Cobra* sitting a short distance away. "That is my fighter . . . the best fighter in the Russian Air Force. If you wish, you can fly."

"The colonel," Yurasov continued, noting that Zhuk was finished speaking, "would like to feed you and your men in true Russian style. The colonel says there will be plenty of vodka, plenty of good . . ." Yurasov paused and thought, unable to translate a particular word into English. After a few seconds he gave up and asked Zhuk a question and Zhuk gave off an enormous laugh.

"Pussy," Zhuk said. "You like pussy, no?"

"Pussy?" said Sutton and turned to Yurasov. "I'm afraid I don't—"

Zhuk, still laughing, struck an arm out and pointed to a figure in the crowd. "That is pussy, no?"

Griffin smiled. "That's a nurse he's pointing to." He glanced down at the crew. "Gentlemen, the colonel wishes to give his tired American friends a little Russian snapper with our caviar."

Sutton shot a quick disapproving eye at Griffin and said to Yurasov, "Please tell the colonel that we would appreciate anything he offers, that his hospitality is very generous."

Zhuk didn't wait for the translation. "I understand." His smile disappeared and, with a serious tone, he asked Sutton, "Do you know Lana Turner?"

"Lana Turner?"

"Movie star," Zhuk said, annoyed at Sutton's ignorance. "Very beautiful. Do you know her?"

"No, I don't," said Sutton, sensing Zhuk's anger, "but my mother does."

Zhuk was pleased.

Sutton, vodka-dazed, followed a second-story balcony around a neglected courtyard. A couple of mangy dogs lifted their weary heads and yawned in unison. A shuttered window hung open, about to fall off rusted hinges—through a bathroom window Sutton saw a woman's back, naked and smooth, bent over, and heard a gagging sound. He stopped and listened, knocked on a thick bolted door and waited. A moment passed—a weak female responded in Russian.

Her shoes, a pair of Russian combat boots, were

beside the bed, a pair of little doughnut stockings rolled next to her cotton panties. The bathroom door was closed—behind it, more gagging. The cotton panties reminded Sutton of June Westerly. He saw her red hair, thin shoulders, the always sad cocoa brown eyes, her room with the laundry strewn around, the wet panties dangling from a clothes line, artists drawing paper and boxes of colored charcoals and pastels here and there. She said she didn't mind, that her parents were dead before she turned twelve, that she'd served tables in a diner, worked the receptionist's desk at a hospital, made ends meet on her own since she was fourteen. She would make a living painting and drawing, which was the only thing that mattered in her life besides screwing—which she did with a vigor that would knock your fillings out.

Sutton had dated June a dozen times, seen three movies with her, had six lunches, taken nine drives in his car, two flights in his father's crop duster, and spoken to her once and couldn't recall the conversation. The rest of the time they screwed like horses, one of those sweet honest relationships based on sex and nothing else, thank you.

The bathroom door swung open and Griffin stepped out naked with a towel wrapped around his waist and his eyes the color of a pig's snout. Sutton thought he was living a bad dream. "I thought you didn't drink," he said to Griffin.

"Only when I'm drunk," was the thick reply.

The woman's voice, muffled in the linen, spoke something in Russian—which Griffin, Mister Know-It-All, pretended to understand. "She loves me," he said, weaving toward the bed—and before he got there the woman flopped over like a beached seal, a sluggish move that revealed her chubby breasts, her thick patch of reddish hair.

"Jesus," Griffin said, "this is embarrassing, you coming in like this."

"I knocked for Christ's sake. Listen, sport, they're giving us a goddamned feast down there and you're up here screwing your lights out. Let me tell you something, these sons a bitches are revolutionary motherfuckers. They kill people for less than this."

"Hey, you are missing the point. Old Roadblock said we could have a little snapper. On the house. Some *pussy,* he said."

The woman grinned a stupid drunken smirk and reached out and grabbed a corner of Griffin's towel and tried to cover her fiery thatch.

"Aw, bullshit," Sutton said, "you're just an ill-mannered bastard." He checked out the room, scanned the place. The candelabra, the solid oak dresser, the thick bear rug—this must have been a landowner's home, he thought, and these Communist loons took it over, maybe shot them. "They love us. They think we are either gangsters or movie stars. Tutone told Roadblock he was in an Esther Williams movie, and I told him my mother would send him an autographed Lana Turner photo."

"I didn't know your mother knows Lana Turner."

"Yeah, and she knows FDR and Churchill and Stalin. Listen, Roadblock wants to go up in *The Beast* tomorrow. He's an influential bastard. He's well connected to the Party."

"How would you know? Only thing you know is flying banged up airplanes." Griffin stood, swayed, the motion revealing the woman's patch again, much to Sutton's delight. The woman, booze-eyed, hunched up on an elbow and watched Griffin dash for the bathroom, banging the door, slipping and crashing against the tub. She grinned, cocked her head to listen: a spewing sound, the flop of thick liquid hitting porcelain, and then more groaning. The woman's eyes rolled in their little fatty sockets and she giggled, flopped back on the bed and folded her hands neatly across her soft breasts.

Sutton sauntered into the bathroom, filled with American toiletries, and he picked up a bottle of lime aftershave and studied the label. "You don't look too good. You should have something to eat. They have vodka, caviar, Scotch, smoked salmon—they even have reindeer meat—stuff you haven't seen in months."

Griffin groaned again and Sutton said, "Better practice your drinking routine." Griffin grabbed a pitcher of water, flushed the tub clean. Sutton tried to unscrew the bottle. "Better get dressed and come downstairs, it's not nice to fuck with revolutionaries."

"I do what I feel like doing." Griffin slowly pushed up from the floor, motioned toward the door. "Call her in here."

"What for?" Sutton dabbed his face with the cologne.

"She's a nurse."

"Listen," Sutton said, combing his hair, "these guys love us. Maybe they're bullshitting, but the way I feel right now, I could use some bullshit. Parker was supposed to be the guest of honor and when he hears about this orgy, he's going to go bananas." Sutton eyed the walls, the tub. "Speaking of bananas, what the hell have you been eating?"

Griffin took a sip of water, turned and walked into the bedroom and threw himself on the bed. The woman had her hair in her mouth and a drunken empty smile on her face. "Some buddy," Griffin said, looking down at the woman's short body and patted her stomach and belched. "They don't do it like American women. They move like seals in the water. It is truly weird. Shit, I can't explain it."

"Maybe you should do it again," Sutton said, studying himself in the mirror, "just to get the hang of it before Parker court-martials all of us."

"Court-martial? For what, for cripes sake?"

"Unauthorized fucking."

"Jeez," Griffin said, sounding a little amazed. "I never thought of that. But, what the hell, I made my choice. To tell the truth, if it comes to that I'll back my ass into a spinning prop. Fuck 'em."

"Good decision. That's the spirit," Sutton said, weaving, slurring his words, feeling like he had a bag full of muffins in his mouth. The woman turned, threw her stubby arms around Griffin's neck, and waved Sutton away with a contemptuous motion. He felt dismissed, unwanted, and turned and walked out. Sutton slammed the door and heard the shutter crash against the floor—an instant later the sky ignited a fiery orange and the ground erupted from the shock of a terrible explosion.

The two Luftwaffe He 111 bombers stabbed the night sky over Poltava at a 25° angle, their 660 horsepower BMW in-line engines screaming as they dove toward the Russian airfield. These were the same type German bombers that were the first over Warsaw years ago, and the bombers shot down in the greatest numbers during the Battle of Britain. In victory and in defeat they were notable—their smooth lines and 82-foot elliptical wings sliced downward as their pilots aimed for a single brilliant glow in the center of the airfield. Moments ago another He 111—code-named *Nightstar* by German mission planners—had tobogganed down from the cloudless night and simultaneously released two target-identification bombs filled with 72 pounds of Hematite spotting charge, a ferric oxide compound. With nose-fuse detonation great billowing clouds of red smoke spread out in the shape of a baseball diamond; the second bomb, an incendiary, contained 25 pounds of Photoflash powder that produced 500 million candle-power of bright, almost blinding white light. The combination set the airfield off under a blood-red haze, casting the American and Russian ships in ghostly vermillion shapes.

The two diving He 111s—code-name *Helldiver*—released clusters of incendiary bombs packed with Magnesium-Thermite that further illuminated the target. The airfield was now flooded in a dome of light enveloping the sky above for several thousand feet. At full throttle the He 111s sped off into the darkness, their part of the raid successfully completed. After their departure a gaggle of 60 Ju 88s and He 111s began their bombing runs.

The first salvo of bombs tossed Sutton back against the wall of the balcony. Chunks of shrapnel and rock peppered the wall above his head as he sprawled out on the floor.

The German bombers were swimming down from 13,000 feet, a wide spiral a mile in diameter. Usually disciplined, tonight the German pilots' excitement had overcome them and they were like a pack of loose sharks. The group was commanded by *Oberst* Jurgen Becker, the son of a farmer and an accomplished bomber pilot who had survived eighty-six combat missions during the Battle of Britain. Since late that afternoon when the reconnaissance aircraft spotted the American bombers, Becker had to make hasty but precise plans for this raid—because never again would the Germans have the opportunity to destroy such a large force of aircraft.

Despite instruments and sophisticated gear, a flier relied on the tug and pull of gravity on his guts and inner ear, the dangers his eyes telegraphs to the brain. The things a flier did not see were as important to him as the things he did see—a fighter coming toward him without gunsmoke trailing behind was not firing his guns and was therefore not a threat. There were subtle actions that fliers read instantly, that say positive or negative things, subtleties that are not taught in school. Most of all, fliers like Sutton were at home in the air, not on the ground.

When Sutton looked up, Griffin had his pants buckled and his shirt on his back; he was shoeless, crouched over, as he made his way toward Sutton.

"Where's the nurse?" Sutton shouted above the thumping bombs.

"Gone," said Griffin, sliding across the floor, "out the rear staircase in five seconds flat."

213

"They must be used to this."

Along the runway the incessant tempo of explosions shook the earth, coming in twos and threes, then a lull, then three and four more terrific bangs, each blast igniting the air and shedding a continuous glow of light.

Sutton looked up. Parts of aircraft were spinning downward. Human figures were caught, frozen by the bright light, and then vanished. The sharp odor of cordite filled the air.

The thrust of the attack was aimed at the airfield, clearly marked by flares and incendiaries. *Oberst* Becker, his neck wrapped neatly in a white silk scarf, had calculated two hours' fuel time over the target, and he was determined to remain there to the minute—until each bomber had effectively released its load. He swept in from the north at 6,000 feet, toggled a cluster of 500 pounders, then pulled back sharply, banking left at full throttle. He glanced out through the canopy and watched the bombs detonate on the airfield. This was an opportunity few bomber pilots would encounter— the chance to bomb the enemy unopposed, as if they were engaged in a practice run over some sleepy meadow.

Along the flightline, around the American and Russian bombers and fighters, Russian airmen scurried for cover. Within thirty yards of each explosion, men were shredded. The fiery explosions flipped trucks end over end thirty feet into the air, a playful configuration, but hideous in the confusion. Some men were moving and screaming, wandering aimlessly without limbs. Some didn't scream; they walked slowly with a dead-eyed stare. Walls and windows were blown out, the concussions deafening the inhabitants. Through the dark countryside, horses hugging stone walls were felled like sacks of rye.

Sutton and Griffin remained on the balcony, checking their watches every few minutes, giving up after an hour while the *Luftwaffe* went about their business.

"Not very pleasant on this end, is it?" said Sutton.

"What? I can't hear you."

"I said, it's not very pleasant on this end. Now you know what it feels like to be on the receiving end of things. Sort of puts things in a different light, doesn't it?"

"I don't know which is worse—getting shot at up there or getting bombed on down here."

"I think I'd rather be down here," Sutton said.

"Why?"

"You can't crash."

The bombing lasted two hours, terminating at 0115. *Oberst* Becker reformed his bombers and headed them toward their home base with cheers of joy and congratulations filling their headsets. Before they landed, each airman that had flown that evening was certain that the mission was an outstanding success— one of the most notable for the *Luftwaffe* during the entire war.

Sutton and Griffin never left the balcony throughout the entire attack. Griffin, with his eyes closed most of the time, spoke quietly, and as each word came out of his mouth, his hands shook like someone suffering a terrible pain. He told Sutton that he didn't think he could go on any longer in the war, that he was so damned scared he felt like crying. And then he admitted something Sutton thought he'd never hear him admit.

"Remember the loop I did," Griffin said. "Well, someone else took the ship up before me and tested it out. A week before I flew the loop, my dad wanted me to test out the *Aerohound* and I told him I couldn't do it. I told him I didn't have the guts to test it out. So, they got someone else, I don't know who. But now I know something about myself that I never knew before—I don't have the guts to go on. All my life I led myself to believe that I was different, that I was some kind of hero. I started to believe what the press wrote about me. Half that stuff was fed to them by my father." Griffin opened his eyes and looked at Sutton. "What am I going to do? I'm so damned scared I think I'm going to die."

Sutton could have told him that it was he who flew the loop; he could have told him that before he took the *Aerohound* up he went behind the barn and vomited, and that he could hardly keep his hands from shaking just before he flew the maneuver. He could have told Griffin to quit, to have Parker declare that Roger Griffin was unfit for combat. But Sutton didn't tell him any of these things; he just said, "Keep your eyes closed and in a few minutes this will all be over."

Because Sutton knew that if he told Griffin the truth, if he told him to quit, it would hurt him more than the damned bombs they both dreaded.

Tutone and the rest of *The Beast*'s crew were caught in the dining room where the banquet was being given in their honor. Along with their Russian hosts, their first indication of attack came when the glass windows were blown out. Most of the Russian personnel—

including Colonel Zhuk—dashed for the flightline. Many were never seen again.

At morning's first light the full damage of the raid was assessed and it was worse than imagined.

Of the 73 American B-17s caught on the ground, 47 were destroyed; six were repairable and would need spare parts flown in from England; four were fixable the next day. One of those was *The Beast*.

SEVENTEEN

"Will it fly?" Tutone asked Sergeant Holden.

"Of course it will fly," Holden said, patting *The Beast*'s nose, the first kind gesture Tutone had ever seen Holden perform. "We took a few parts here, a few parts there, added a little glue, and the old bitch is reborn again."

The Chief stood next to Tutone, inspecting the lines of his ship like a jeweler checking out an expensive diamond.

Holden said, "Meet with your approval, Chief?"

"I won't believe it until it gets off the ground," the Chief replied sternly.

"Shit," Holden said, "that won't happen unless you guys take 'er off instead of staring and asking a lot of dumb questions."

In an hour they would be in the air. Colonel Zhuk would fly in the copilot's seat while Sutton showed him the controls. Griffin sat quietly in the jump seat, listening to Zhuk's childish questions, most of which had nothing to do with flying or technique.

"How much this cost?" he asked, referring to the B-17.

Sutton threw out a figure—over $200,000—and Zhuk needed a translation into Russian currency, a process that killed five minutes while everyone tried to explain the currency difference.

"Tell me about Cadillac and Buick cars," said Zhuk to Sutton.

While this wore on, the war did not stop and the rest of the crew was occupied with scanning the sky for German fighters, a threat that was very real. An hour later they circled Poltava and Zhuk inspected the damage from two thousand feet and then called the tower and told them to announce over the airfield's loudspeaker that he was piloting the B-17. Halfway down on final approach, Sutton took the controls sensing that Zhuk was trying to fly this huge bomber in the same manner he would a nimble fighter.

When the wheels touched the repaired runway, Russian airmen tossed up their hats and cheered. Tutone, never at loss for words, pressed his interphone button. "Three cheers for old Roadblock."

Not far away the gravediggers were still busy.

The last propeller jerked still, and Parker walked to *The Beast*. Zhuk and Sutton dropped from the forward hatch. Tutone was the first crewman out.

"Good landing," Parker said to Tutone, watching him unzip his jacket.

"Good landing? Captain Sutton's landings are all

good, Colonel."

"Sutton? I thought that was Zhuk."

"Pretend," said Tutone. "Just pretend it was. You'll make the old guy feel like a true hero of the Russian people."

"Congratulations," Parker said, shaking Zhuk's hand. "Marvelous landing."

Yurasov translated, having arrived just in time from halfway across the field, out of breath but catching Parker's last words like a baseball player making a spectacular save.

"The colonel," Yurasov said, "wishes to get even with the Germans and would like to launch a heavy offensive as soon as possible."

Parker smiled, one of those deceptive Parker grins. "Please tell the colonel," he said, speaking through Yurasov, "that our strength is cut in half and that according to our latest intelligence reports there is a danger that this airbase could be overrun by German Waffen-SS troops as soon as tomorrow afternoon."

Zhuk, with displeased eyes glaring, spoke rapidly in Russian to Yurasov while Parker, after quickly greeting Sutton, said in a whisper, "Colonel Zhuk wants to bomb the Germans."

"That's wonderful," Sutton said with a fake smile.

"Colonel Parker," Yurasov said, "Colonel Zhuk is not afraid of the Germans. He says they would not dare attack this airbase, that they are outnumbered by brave Russian troops. He also says that you must be getting inaccurate intelligence reports and would, instead, with all due respect, rely on the intelligence reports of Russian officers."

"Well, it is certainly something to consider. Tell the

Colonel that I will have to assess the damage first and will then report to him about the availability of my B-17s."

Zhuk seemed pleased and smiled. He said, "Russian fliers will fly escort for American friends, and if American fliers have no planes to fly they will fly Russian bombers."

"Well . . . well, thanks," said Parker.

Everyone shook hands and Zhuk turned and left.

The Russian bomber sat at the far end of the airfield. Similar in appearance to the American B-26, the Tupolev Tu-2 had an olive-green upper surface and a light gray undersurface. Classified as an attack bomber with a normal crew of four, the Tu-2 had two 1,850 horsepower ASh-82FN 14-cylinder, two-row radial engines. Wing span was sixty-one feet, length forty-five feet. By any standard, the Tu-2 was no slouch in the air. It had a maximum speed of 343 miles per hour with an initial climb of 2,300 feet per minute. Service ceiling was over 31,000 feet. Armament was typically three manually aimed 12.7mm Beresin BS machine guns—one in the upper rear of the crew compartment, which was covered with a long metal-framed bubble canopy; one in the rear dorsal position and one in the rear ventral position. It also had two 20mm ShVAK cannons, each with 200 rounds and fixed in the wing roots for ground attack. The bomb bay was equipped to hold a maximum load of 5,000 pounds.

To express his confidence in the American fliers, that afternoon Colonel Zhuk "requested" Sutton and two other crewmen from *The Beast* to fly a single-plane mission against German ground forces 150 miles south of Poltava. "To show you," in Zhuk's words, "what metal Russian fliers are made of."

Sutton would fly in the copilot's seat, with Zhuk acting as command pilot in the left seat. Tutone, anxious to get back in the air no matter what ship he was flying in, would man the machine gun in the rear of the cockpit, and the Chief the gun in the dorsal position. The ship was configured with a 2,000-pound bomb load—which would be secondary to the strafing run Zhuk had hastily formulated in the remains of his Flight Operations office undergoing reconstruction now as the crew assembled.

Parker, not willing to antagonize his superiors back in England, decided to allow his men to fly with Zhuk. Tutone immediately expressed enthusiasm. Sutton, somewhat leery at first, was curious about the Tu-2's flight characteristics and was somewhat overcome by the opportunity to fly something different than the B-17. He would chalk it up as a new adventure. Aside from the normal risk, there wasn't much to fear about the Tu-2, an aircraft that was undoubtedly one of the outstanding designs of World War II. It was formidable and reliable in service, extremely popular with Russian airmen and barely needed any modifications in the course of a long career that would extend through the Berlin Airlift.

"I hate to admit it," Sutton said to Tutone and the Chief, standing under the nose section, "but it doesn't look bad at all." That was half the battle, because if an airplane looked good on the ground it most often behaved well in the air.

The Tu-2 had a red rose painted on the fuselage

under the cockpit on the pilot's side—the rose was Zhuk's personal insignia. The ship had a factory-fresh appearance, as did Zhuk's *King Cobra,* both ships getting meticulous attention from their maintenance crews. The large spinners on each engine were painted blood red, which matched the color of the Russian national emblems on the fuselages and wings, and there was just a trace of exhaust stains on the nacelles.

The ship gave off an air of trustworthiness that even the Chief could not deny. "I hope you're right," he said to Sutton.

"Hey, look," Tutone said filing his nails, motioning to the maintenance men pulling the wheel chocks away, "those guys aren't going to let their boss up in a bucket of crap. The bird looks solid to me. What about you, Chief?"

The Chief, busy squeezing his new leather flying jacket, shook his head, a rendering of the seal of approval. "It's not *The Beast.*"

Tutone blew nail dust from his fingers. "On the whole, the Russians ain't bad pilots," he said without looking up. "But they can't win the entire war without help. How do you feel about it, boss?"

Sutton was thinking of T.R. and Tutone's question brought him back. "How do I think about the Russians needing help? Who knows?"

The Chief gave a few more powerful squeezes on his jacket then threw it over his shoulders and slipped his arms in. "I don't know whether I'm going to like this or hate this," he said.

"The airplane?" asked Tutone, looking up from his nails.

"No, the jacket."

Zhuk arrived and the maintenance people, more formal than their American counterparts, stood at attention and saluted. The man in charge of the silent group gave a quick verbal update on the status of the ship. Then Zhuk spun around heavily and greeted the three Americans.

EIGHTEEN

The air above the earth was a blue porcelain dome. For a moment Sutton was taken away from Zhuk's fingers tapping the fuel gauges, an unsettling experience. He peered through the glass canopy, a miniature hothouse up here at 15,000 feet with the two 14-cylinder engines throbbing evenly. In a B-17, Sutton only had a limited field of view; but in here, the view was wider and the sky seemed larger. It brought back the days of flying in an open cockpit plane when he could see without limitation. It was free of the sense of claustrophobia he felt in *The Beast*'s cockpit, nailed in there in his flying suit, plugged in, attached, surrounded by dials and gauges, levers and switches. The feeling here in the Tu-2 was much more open, more unattached to the ship itself.

They had been in the air for forty-five minutes when the engines surged, palsied, then toned down. Sutton's stomach filled with that horrible sinking sensation, and he looked over at Zhuk. He would read Zhuk's face, not the instruments, because they were in undecipherable Russian. So it was Zhuk's face that took their place, and now it seemed calm, the bear's eyes reflecting no sense of emergency. Instead, Zhuk pointed down to an area ahead, perhaps fifty miles south in line with their heading. He had nosed the ship over and now they were losing altitude, the altimeter needle spinning backward quickly, Zhuk's big gloved hands holding the control wheel forward in his lap.

"Waffen-SS," Zhuk said, pointing again. "German troops. We bomb . . . strafe like this—" His left hand was palms up, indicating the ground, and the right was the Tu-2 coming along the palm at what seemed to be fifty feet off the ground. "Have you ever strafed troops?" Zhuk asked.

Sutton shook his head.

Zhuk unsnapped his oxygen mask and revealed a big smile. "Fun," he said. "We fly low, shoot big cannons." He pointed to the armaments panel, then toggled the 20mm ShVAK switch; the guns were ready for firing. At 8,000 feet, Zhuk nosed the ship over further until it was almost in a vertical dive and increased the power setting.

"How fast?" asked Sutton, pointing to the airspeed indicator.

"Three hundred and fifty."

Sutton raised his eyebrows.

"And still much power left," Zhuk added proudly, nudging the throttle ahead slightly. The engine tone rose, a sweet smooth powerful sound. "Here," Zhuk said, handing Sutton a pair of captured German binoculars.

Sutton scanned the ground ahead, picked out Zhuk's target—a German camp not yet suspecting the approach of Russian aircraft.

The Tu-2 dipped further and further down and without looking at the altimeter, Sutton estimated their height aloud into the interphone: "We're about fifty feet off the ground."

Tutone let out a whoop of joy. "Go get 'em Roadblock!"

On the ground, an *SS-Hauptsturmfuhrer* attached to the Fourth SS-Panzer Corps, stepped away from a Kubelwagon and lifted a canteen of water to his parched lips. One of his freshly polished boots was on the fender; his tunic, drying in the sunlight, hung from the car's outside mirror. As the cool water passed through his lips he glanced at the sky and reacted instantly. "Air attack! Run for cover!" Next he saw the bright muzzle flashes coming off the wing root cannons of Zhuk's speeding ship. The canteen dropped to the ground.

Zhuk's thumb hit the red firing button and paused there. Sutton, off the binoculars now, saw the puffs of dust and rock as the cannon shells bounced off the ground, two lines converging on the lone figure without a shirt.

"Jesus," Sutton said aloud.

From the time Zhuk fired to the time the shirtless figure dropped, less than two seconds elapsed. When the SS officer dropped the canteen, his next motion was catlike as he sprang for the cover of the car, perhaps eight feet away. Before he took two steps a 20mm shell slammed into his lower back and severed him with blinding force. Two rounds struck the car, igniting the fuel tank and sending the vehicle up into the air and over on its side.

The Tu-2 came in so low and so fast that none of the German troops had time to aim or fire their weapons. As the ship passed over them the Chief opened fire with his ventral machine gun, watching the dirt kick up in his wake.

Zhuk pulled up quickly at full throttle and kicked hard left rudder and the ship zoomed around on its port wing tip. "Good, no?" he asked.

"Great!" shouted Tutone.

Zhuk said, "We go back, okay?"

"Okay," said Sutton.

But before they came halfway around the Tu-2 engines choked, backfired, and a long plume of black smoke spit from the Number 2 engine. The ship lost speed like a roller coaster plowing through a pool of water.

"What the hell was that?"

"Hey," Tutone said, calmly. "Hey, boss, I think I'm—"

"Shut up, Benny, something's wrong!"

Zhuk's face went sour. The bear's eyes showed concern. "We are hit!"

"Feather the Number Two engine!" said Sutton instinctively, watching Zhuk's hands working the controls. Sutton looked outside and saw the engine come to a halt.

As they passed over the German camp Zhuk already

had the bomb bay doors opened and salvoed his load.

"Boss, I think I'm hit!"

Sutton turned in his seat and looked at Tutone.

Tutone's face was the color of the rose painted on the ship.

Zhuk motioned Sutton back toward Tutone then began jabbering into the radio, notifying Poltava that their commander was flying a damaged aircraft.

Sutton unplugged himself and opened Tutone's flight jacket.

Tutone was muttering: "One minute . . . everything okay . . . then . . . I think I'm going to get sick."

"Just stay calm, you'll be all right, do you hear me, stay calm!"

"I never thought I'd die in Russia. I thought maybe France, or Germany, or maybe England, but never Russia—"

"I said shut up!"

Sutton had the jacket opened. Tutone's shirt was covered with blood.

"What happened?" the Chief asked.

"Benny's hit. Colonel, how far to Poltava—how much flying time?"

Colonel Zhuk shrugged his shoulders.

The Chief asked, "How bad is he?"

Sutton ripped open Tutone's shirt. "He's hit under the collarbone. Lots of blood."

"Is it spurting?"

"No."

"Is the bone broken? If the bone's broken it could have gone into his—"

"Shut up! I'm doing my best!"

231

Tutone opened his eyes. "Lousy break. I thought I'd die somewhere else, not here."

"Listen," Sutton said, applying pressure to a point on Tutone's neck and holding a scarf over the wound, "you're not dying."

"Who said?" Tutone asked.

NINETEEN

With one engine out the Tu-2 began to lose altitude—not a drastic loss but the ground was coming up at a perceptible rate. Zhuk, hunched over the controls, concentrated on his course. They were six minutes out of Poltava, flying along on one good engine, when they felt the bang. Sutton thought that it was a direct hit by a flak shell.

At 20,000 feet the cold temperature would have condensed the fuel particles in the Tu-2's fuel tank, making it highly inflammable. But the ship flew on at 6,000 feet. Normal temperatures caused the fuel-air mixture to be rich and thus not as volatile if they were higher. The ragged vapor fire trailing aft of the damaged engine was not a threat until one of the engine's brace bolts, red hot, ripped lose and punctured the fuel tank. This was the explosion Sutton had heard. Until that moment the fuel would have burned away melting some of the alloy fabric and the wing spars and dissipating itself safely.

The explosion shattered much of the canopy and heaved Sutton against the fold-down seat Tutone had used until he was wounded. The rudder pedals and control column were momentarily wrenched from Zhuk's hands. The Chief was not certain what had happened, but Sutton had been expecting such a blast.

When the 85-gallon fuel tank exploded it broke the wing at the starboard engine. Simultaneously it fractured the engine's main girder at the point of attachment to the wing and broke the major support beam at the wing's leading edge. Without support, the dead engine began to buffet violently, and fifteen seconds later it tore itself off the engine. The Tu-2 continued for a minute, almost normally, but rising slightly away from the lack of weight. Now, the ship was totally out of balance and nothing Zhuk could do would save her. It was a falling mass of steel and useless parts. It continued to tilt down toward the good engine, which still hummed along perfectly. The ailerons were ineffective, their control cables apparently severed by the explosion. Sutton watched thunderstruck as the green earth appeared over the top of the canopy. The ship had spiraled over in a slow corkscrew turn. "Don't panic!" Sutton yelled out to Zhuk. "For God's sake, don't panic!"

Sutton had checked his parachute clip then reached for Tutone's; both were clipped on. He knew the roll would continue faster and faster until centrifugal force made it impossible to bail out. Already his arms were flung over his head and then the whole weight of his body pressed against the cockpit floor as the ship came around a second time. Grasping the edge of the trunking around the throttle controls, he pushed himself away from the floor, pulling on Tutone's shoulder harness with all his strength. The canopy had already been flung open by Zhuk, preparing to bail out also.

Using his muscular legs and pinning his broad shoulders against the canopy railing, Sutton heaved himself away. The effort surprised him because it didn't require the strength he anticipated. This was because the ship was over on its back again, falling in a shallow dive. Inch by inch and using every ounce of strength his body could give out, he pushed away. He was clear but something seemed caught. The twisted metal braces and ragged glass on the canopy had snagged every belt, harness and wire plug on Tutone's half-conscious body. Exhausted and sweating, he gave one last kick against the fuselage and fell free, pulling Tutone with him.

At first he felt elated, flattened in the air and falling. Then he realized that unless he pulled the D-ring on the parachute he would splatter on the ground in less than ninety seconds. He kicked himself into the strong slipstream that smashed at him like a baseball bat. But he was also surprised at himself because he had been in plenty of spins flying his father's planes around the countryside in upstate New York. This was different though; he had no control of the ship, and he was falling through the air gripping another man's parachute harness.

As the curving fall continued, both he and Tutone were spinning head over heels until the energy of the motion tucked them into a folded position. He recalled that you must not open your chute like this, that you had to wait until your body stopped spinning. But the spinning continued, and this perhaps was the cause of his growing panic. He knew the damned ground was coming up at 120 miles per hour and nothing but the parachute canopy would slow it down. For a second he thought about saving himself, about releasing Tutone and not worrying about pulling the other man's D-ring. The wait seemed the longest in his life—and then he yanked Tutone's D-ring and watched the canopy lines unravel and tumble out of the green backpack. Tutone slowed and the distance between them grew and the canopy blossomed.

Then Sutton did something stupid—he kicked out, realizing it had no effect at all. He reached for his own D-ring and pulled. Nothing happened. The strength in his hand, the one he used to pull Tutone away from the falling bomber, had been expended. He pulled with his other hand and the lines spilled out and the canopy opened. A second before it did he shouted two words: "God, please!" As he settled down through the air he looked around and saw three more chutes, and four miles to the north he spotted the unmistakable shape of Poltava.

At five that afternoon Sergeant Holden entered Colonel Parker's makeshift office wearing a new leather flight jacket. Parker, sitting behind an old Hungarian desk, looked up from a teletype message. Sutton and Griffin sat nearby.

Parker said, "Is it my imagination, or am I seeing a lot of new jackets since we landed here?"

Holden, with a big grin, said, "No, sir, it's not your imagination."

"Well, where the hell are all these new jackets coming from?" asked Parker.

"Sir," Sergeant Holden told Parker, "some of the men brought them from England."

"What for?"

"The Russians," Sutton said. "The men heard that the Russians would take jackets, cigarettes, and watches."

"They heard," said Griffin, "that we could use them as barter, and they were correct."

"And what do we get in return?" Parker asked the group. Then, without waiting for a reply, he said, "Never mind, I think I know. What is it, Sergeant?"

"Sir, the doctor says Tutone will be all right."

Parker thanked Holden and waited until he left the room and then he held up the teletype message. "That's great news but, gentlemen, this isn't. It's a top secret message from Colonel Hayes at Wing; it arrived a half hour ago. It seems that our intelligence reports are accurate, that the Germans are on their way here. They could be at this airbase in less than twelve hours."

"Well," Sutton said, lighting a cigarette, "we're not going to remain here, are we?"

"No. As a matter of fact the message orders us to prepare to leave."

"For where?" Griffin asked, sitting on the edge of his chair.

"Another Russian airbase—a place called Morova

about two hours' flying time from here. So, that's that."
Parker put the message down on the center of the desk
and folded his thin hands and looked up at Sutton.
"We will fly the undamaged Forts out and load them
up with the crews from the ships that can't fly. I want
everyone ready to leave"—he checked his watch—"in
one hour. Is that understood?"

"Yes," said Sutton, standing.

"Oh, there's one other thing," Parker said. His eyes
rolled up to the ceiling and his face changed; it looked
pained and his body went still, as if overcome by a
sudden chill; something difficult was about to come out
of his mouth. "There's no guarantee that the Germans
won't be at Morova when we arrive. Apparently they're
on a big offensive. It might last a day, it might last a
week, no one knows for sure. At any rate, that's the
latest."

Sutton and Griffin walked out of the building. The
sun here was different, the clouds were different, even
the air had a strange, unfamiliar scent. Sutton's face
was deeply lined, his eyes were bloodshot and when he
brought the cigarette up to his lips Griffin saw his
fingers shaking.

They walked toward *The Beast* in silence, and before
they were a hundred yards away they stopped and
looked at their old ship. A soft breeze drew Sutton's
brown hair down over his eyes and he remembered the
first time he saw *The Beast*. She had changed, too, like
all of them, and if she was wiser she was also battered
and worn. Time and battle had taken away her youth.
When Sutton looked at her he looked at himself, and
he felt something that he could not describe to anyone,
that he would never even try to explain as long as he

lived. *The Beast* sat there dormant but somehow it achieved a life that only certain special objects could have. In the moments, in the years ahead, he would never feel like this again.

"We'd better get going," Griffin said quietly.

"Yeah, sure," said Sutton, "off again on the wings of death."